I0668073

BUNNY HAMMOND

The Heartless Ranch Is Haunted - First Edition

Nothing Is Ever Really Gone

First published by Publish Drive 2025

Copyright © 2025 by Bunny Hammond

All rights reserved. No part of this publication may be reproduced, stored or transmitted in any form or by any means, electronic, mechanical, photocopying, recording, scanning, or otherwise without written permission from the publisher. It is illegal to copy this book, post it to a website, or distribute it by any other means without permission.

This novel is entirely a work of fiction. The names, characters and incidents portrayed in it are the work of the author's imagination. Any resemblance to actual persons, living or dead, events or localities is entirely coincidental.

Bunny Hammond asserts the moral right to be identified as the author of this work.

Bunny Hammond has no responsibility for the persistence or accuracy of URLs for external or third-party Internet Websites referred to in this publication and does not guarantee that any content on such Websites is, or will remain, accurate or appropriate.

Designations used by companies to distinguish their products are often claimed as trademarks. All brand names and product names used in this book and on its cover are trade names, service marks, trademarks and registered trademarks of their respective owners. The publishers and the book are not associated with any product or vendor mentioned in this book. None of the companies referenced within the book have endorsed the book.

First edition

This book was professionally typeset on Reedsy.
Find out more at reedsy.com

To my husband, the light of my life.

To my daughters, with all my love.

To my brother, I set out to make you into a self published author and made myself into one instead.

To my parents.

And to my in-law's.

To all the millennial women I know.

To old friends, acquaintances and new friends everywhere.

To Kerri and Darcie and Angie and Kristina. To Abby and Kelsey, Liz, Anna and Ruth. To Elizabeth, Mary and Emmalee, to Samantha, Marissa and Katee, to Akiko, and Delores, Jeanie and Geneva.

Contents

Foreword

This is a made up story, therefore I promise you it will end better than most of the true stories did.

Also, I know many people named Don- and Barb and Brian and Allan and so on. Character names were chosen from census data of most common names. Any resemblance to actual people is strictly coincidental but I do extend you all my warmest wishes.

I

Part One

1

The Heartless Is Haunted

Tall stubborn stems of red grass, rust and auburn like harsh words.

The Heartless Ranch, Nebraska
   March of 2025

When people said the Heartless Ranch was haunted, they were right. He was the solitary shadow, the rustle, the watching eyes that people felt. The blue listener and the sudden bursts of laughter during the full moon. For him, the secrets of the Heartless Ranch had never died.

The Heartless Ranch stretched from just east of Dismal, north of the highway to just west of the Hammond's summer range. The decrepit buildings stood on a ridge above a flat piece of hard ground that had been plowed during the Homestead Act. You could still see the outlines of where the cuts had been made. The land didn't forget and the ghost liked it here.

Tonight he stretched out his hand to brush the grass as he walked. Tall stubborn stems of red grass, rust and auburn like harsh words.

As he walked, the wind picked up. The clouds high above him scudded across the endless sky. The valley around him was a bowl overflowing with liquid moonlight and the air felt calm to him and thick with something to prove, like a dangerous gunfighter coming out to play with the laws of potential and kinetic energy.

Slender golden stems, dark wheat yellow and light sparkly yellow like our ideas of the moon.

Dry lightning struck this piece of ground some forty times a year. Mostly the locals accepted that Clara County weather was what it was. The strikes were never on the neighboring properties, just the old Heartless ranch. During the dry times the threat of a grass fire starting made people nervous, it had happened occasionally. The county sheriff used to drive out to look around but he didn't do that anymore. No one commented on the change because no one wanted to know. He was a near sighted man, Dismal didn't expect a whole lot from the law anyway.

Bunch grass, all the colors of dark taupe and bright greige like herds of grazing horses that make time stand still. The light got caught here and clung like raindrops to the blades, slowly dripping down. This was the grass that grew in the wounds and he found it the most beautiful. There were no animals here to graze the flat below the house and so the grass remained tall.

Season after season it swayed in the prairie wind and trembled in the silent stillness.

As the spirit wandered across the grassy flat the horses in the distance watched him carefully. These were the neighbor's horses, grazing the far edge of their pasture, in search of mischief in the dropping barometric pressure. A big gray swiveled his ears and stomped his feet as the spirit meandered in the distance. They had seen the apparition many times before. A little dun kept her big liquid eyes on him, as his image began to quiver and shudder sideways unnaturally, she turned her head sharply. The ghost melted out of view, like he was caught in static or high winds that only he could feel, then he solidified again- much closer to the herd. Thunder cracked and broke directly overhead. The big gray spun and kicked with both hind feet and the dun struck at the sky with a sharp whinny. The little remuda tore off along the fence line, manes streaking out in the night air behind them. Time goes on.

The young cowboy grinned solemnly in the dark, he had always liked horses, well- he had always liked broncs. He couldn't hear the hooves anymore.

He turned slowly on his heel to survey back over the way he had come. These were long nights. There used to be so much more going on around here.

The working pens had been good, with a load out on nice hard ground and a short little gravel drive up onto the highway. The perfect place to put cattle on trucks. Even the neighbors had used it. The surrounding pastures narrowed in to some long pens tucked in behind tree groves, so many of the best cattle drives had ended right here. He could hear the cattle bellering, the trucks letting off the air brakes, men shouting. Success and adrenaline were in the air, that part never changed. He could see the horses, the women with long hair braided down their back, the children, the working dogs flitting around the back of the herd in the dust. Of course the glittering semis, the pickups and trailers, that had all been way after him. Things had been done differently in his day. He had been right here to see the end of his era and then remained to see where it was all going. Still this had always been a useful little place, handy and productive.

The skin around his cheekbones fell, golden memories shifting to disgust and regret. The working pens were lying on the ground, the long pens were filled with weeds from last season, the field on the flat next to the house had always been a horse pasture. No one tried to keep cattle or horses around the place anymore. They shied at every shadow, spooked at every sound, a soft breeze could cause hysteria and violent accidents. The old Heartless Ranch was haunted, and the spirit of the young man was alone.

Some nights he tried to leave, as if he had something to prove to God. He reached out a spirit hand to test the boundary and lightening struck the fence line viciously. In that moment he felt almost human as the pain tore over him in waves then it passed. The ghost laughed, unperturbed by the sizzling and crackling continuing all along the barbed wire. Not tonight then, he was bound to this place, fenced in by obligations he couldn't begin to resolve there would be no escape for him. He would wait, new frontiers were coming and one of these days his time would be here again.

A narrow grove of petite trees stood next to the field, these trees had been hand planted in delicate rows, like an orchard. A labor of love gifted to the people of the future. Over time more trees had grown up outside of the pattern, cedars, elms, even a few ponderosas. Man made planning starting to be reclaimed by rugged nature, dead branches big and small littered the ground around the neat rows like fallen bodies in the grass. This was Don's second favorite haunt.

The dark crooked trees stood out in sharp contrast against the light colors of the grasses swaying softly all around. The dark and the light, the hard and the soft, it was beautiful. His brow bone was knitted darkly over his spirit eyes under his hat. He was the only one left. As his forefinger casually brushed the tree, as it had the grass, a thick gouge was made in the tree. Everyone he had ever loved, all of his family, had gone on and left him behind. Another gouge like a shot. The trees here were striped up and down with burns and gouges. He was so much stronger and colder now than he had been in life. Why had God done this to him? Another violent slash in a tree trunk as he ruminated.

A living person could never guess that the damage had been done by the slightest, slowest touch of a spirit hand. A dry lightening storm broke overhead. An explosive current struck the ground in the tree grove, excruciating in it's finality. The ghost never flinched or even looked up. He was used to being powerful by now and he had always been unpredictable. So many things caused him confusion, frustration; anger. God was like lightning, completely controlled and totally inscrutable, all power and pain. It's difficult to philosophize with everything at stake, the consequences come later.

Passersby on the highway at night, if they knew where to look in the distance, could see that the grove of thrashed trees emitted an eerie green glow. No one ever needed to look more closely than from the highway, especially during a lightening storm. Something stalked among those trees. Was it an ancient spirit? Some fearsome piece of native lore? There was nothing like this originating locally. Maybe a spirit from a different region, come to this place for reasons unknown? Something tore into those trees at night like a big cat sharpening their claws. Whatever it was, the collateral damage was real, day or night.

Well, the old Heartless Ranch was haunted after all, not the campfire stories, seasonal tours or investigative television kind, the kind that the locals would say is best not mentioned at all.

The stars conversed overhead and the winds stopped as the night wore on. The young man wandered into the ranch yard to start his nightly rounds. He walked like a man that had been considered cool in his lifetime and in death he was even more distinct. His hat kept his face dark and unreadable at night, the laws of the daytime world didn't apply to him. The light fell around his silhouette differently than the ground around him. Other than that he could be mistaken for a real person. He had been mistaken for a living person many, many times. He smiled to himself. It was too bad the sheriff didn't stop by anymore. He could have used the company.

He started by walking the perimeter and looking at everything closely. The barn was single story, long and low with dark gaping windows and a pair of owls living in it. They turned their heads in unison to watch him stalk by. The old milk shed, the cake shed, the tack room with his saddle rotting on the bottom of the pile, the little building with the cement floor that was good to stack salt in, some collapsed calving sheds, the chicken house with the skunk still living under it. He strolled along.

The old burning barrels, the little shed in the yard that had come in a kit in the 70's, where Gladys had parked her car. Clyde had given that car away after she passed. The shop with the tool bench against the far wall and Clyde's air compressor and arc welder left to rust. Don still thought that had been a shame. The garden pen behind the house near the propane barrel and the clothesline. The fuel barrels with rusted padlocks near the low lean to shed where Clyde's beloved car was still parked. The bunkhouse, stuffed full of junk until the door couldn't swing open, was overrun with mice. Dried up dead horse weeds and ragweed clustered around the buildings and spaces in between them.

Everywhere the ghost strolled he looked at windows and door frames and reached out and rattled doorknobs loudly. The racket he made was punctuated by the picket fence gate slamming shut and creaking open again in the stillness. Finally he came to the open steps down to the cellar, this was the only door he really needed to rattle. The rest was just for show. The metal plate and over sized padlock were showing rust but they held strong as the ghost gave it a good shake. He eyed the door frame and the hinges, old age and rot would be coming one of these days. The moon shone across his smooth clean shaven face, not a day over twenty-two, maybe not even that.

The fateful secret of the Heartless Ranch was safe for one more night. The wind stirred restlessly again. He wandered back up the cement steps to the windmill. He moved with a certain athletic grace, even when he was moping.

Water was pouring out of the lead pipe and the tank was sloshing full, the water gleaming in the moon beams. Swish. Clank. The long silence of death. Swish. Clank. He spent some time listening to the water in every periodic gush and the clang of the pump rod and the clatter of the fan and the tail in the breeze. Windmills connected the underground world to the air and the sky. The rhythmic sound they made reminded him of eternity, always had.

The dedicated Brian Hammond used to shut this windmill off but the wire was found singed and broken again and again. The ghost liked the windmill on and the Hammonds eventually conceded. The spirit smiled when he stood here in front of the windmill- it was nice to be acknowledged in some small way. In many ways this windmill was his monument, his only marker or memorial. He had been killed right here. His mood turned melancholy again as he thought about it, ignored and forsaken. God had sent him back and he had not started any of this.

Where was Joe? Or even Virgil? Or Clyde? He had been their undying protection. The sacrifice, the love of a family, he counted it all as worth it but why was he still here? The windmill tower was covered in little singe marks. He looked longingly down the gravel road past the broken mailbox to the highway. He had tried to leave in so many different ways. He had followed Barb when she left home after her high school graduation. That had not lasted. The ghost nudged a chunk of cement at the base of the tower with his boot toe. Every last one of them had gotten to leave and move on, even the cat had left. His boot left an indention in the concrete.

He adjusted his hat. Maybe he hadn't started it all- but he was the one left to finish it. Freedom wasn't everything. There was still work to be done here and being dead, evidently, did not excuse him. In the memory of a movement picked up from Barb's teenage years he looked ever so briefly up to the heavens. The year was 2025, so far in the future he couldn't even comprehend it. In some ways he was part of this time and place, this modern space-age world, but he could never wrap his mind around the digits. This was 2025. No matter how many decades it took, he would stay until it was over. Don liked to pretend he had a choice.

The picket fence gate swung wildly as Don the ghost wandered up the sidewalk to the front step of the little house with the white siding falling off. This had never been a welcoming house with a front porch, just a big cement step, poured a foot and a half thick and almost four feet wide, and cottonwood trees wrapping close all around. This was where he sat this time of night. He reached for his left front shirt pocket compulsively and silently nodded when he found a pack of cigarettes there. Being a spook was the dangdest thing, Don shook his head as he lit the first one. He had always run through them, so had Clyde- it had been one of the first things they had in common.

Fleeting images of how Clyde had aged flitted through his memory. The way the pale spotted skin had sagged off his face and hung off his neck, the oxygen tanks, the cancer, the cigarettes had brought Clyde low before they killed him. Don the ghost shrugged to himself in the quiet, maybe dying young had had it's advantages. He was going to sit here and smoke this whole pack, he smiled wryly to himself in his own half developed humor.

Now he was thinking about Clyde. The old man had been living alone when the ambulance had come to take him away to the old folks home. Clyde had known he would never be coming back. Don had wondered if he wouldn't be the only ghost anymore. He had stood right here, in the cool shadow of the house, on this cement step, when the EMT's brushed by him carrying the stretcher between them. Clyde had opened his eyes and seen him standing there, leaning on the house in the shadow. Clyde had lifted two fingers to him, in the barest goodbye gesture. Don the ghost would never forget that. He had waited patiently but in the end he was still the only ghost, Clyde must have gone on to heaven. Clyde had been a hard man, conflicted, living out of his element and vulnerable. Don had been there to see it all.

Of course Ivory had gone straight to heaven when she died. She had not lived as long as Clyde did. Don shook his head sadly, she had aged badly. Bitterness had killed her like the cigarettes had killed Clyde, but quicker. In his heart he roamed back to when Ivory had been his wife and dearest companion, his soul mate, back when Ivory had been Ivory. Don the ghost smoked on, his mind lost in imaginary sunshine.

They had been tighter than tight, they had completed each

other more closely than two halves of a whole. Smoke trailed sideways in the night air. They had been happy here together, on this place, in this house. They had been lucky, very lucky, and nothing would ever change that. She had been wild. She had been the heritage of the west incarnated in a woman. She had tried so hard. So many things had come and gone since then but way back there in his haunted memory those golden days still shone, unadulterated. In that way, Ivory would always be Ivory to him.

The ground was starting to have that spring smell that made him think of calving. Ivory and Clyde had calved out a good herd here, every spring. At first the herd had been Herefords, toward the end all black and black white faced cows and calves. She had loved this ranch, that had never changed. Even after she had become a spiteful old lady and started going by her middle name, Gladys, she had loved ranching. He could see her, she wore an overcoat with the front all worn to rags and a decaying wool ear flapper cap that stank as she stalked out with a flash light to check her heavies through glasses as thick as pop bottles. Squelching through the mud and manure in the overshoes with the open buckles, ever in the worst of moods. She had loved calving, loved the springtime with the warmer winds and unpredictable storms. The black brockle faced calves had softened her heart a little this time of year. Don smiled. Then reality pressed in on him again. No one would be calving out a herd here this year, his smile faded. She would have hated to see the place decaying like this, to see what it had all come down to, good thing she had gone straight to heaven. She had deserved to.

When Don the ghost crossed the yard to the lean to shed he caught his boot toe on a piece of scrap iron and fell down. Twenty years ago he would have jumped up quickly, embarrassed that someone might have seen him. But now he took a moment to roll over and get back up, he had no pretense anymore. When he had been alive he could fall backwards off a corral fence and still land on his feet. Or jump astride a bareback horse without a running approach, Ivory had always been impressed with that. In some ways being a spook had taught him humility, the truth was he just wasn't young anymore and he fell down a lot. Ah well, walking wasn't the only way to get around in the spirit world. Don slid through the shed door instead of opening it and there she was, the car that had been Clyde's pride and joy.

She was not a sports car and she was not beautiful. But she was powerful and heavy, gritty and road hungry. She was a 1969 Plymouth Fury III, avocado green with sleek lines for a boat of a car with four doors and a massive trunk. What made her special was what the people around her had put into her, a bond that had bridged the gap between life and death.

Clyde had brought the car home a few years after Barb had left home. Don had never seen him take the time to enjoy something before. Clyde had loved to drive this car, he would put her up on the highway and head west into the setting sun toward Dismal. His intention was rarely to go to town so he never arrived.

Don would ride along in the backseat with his hat tipped to the side, enjoying the scenery and the sunset while Clyde drove for the sheer pleasure of it. He would slow down to look at the grass in the neighbor's pastures, at their cattle and horses, and their windmills and fences and the houses and barns that could be seen from the road. In July, August and Septembers full of regret he would count the stacks and the bales in the hay fields. This was the Sandhills of Nebraska, the land of wet meadows, money and success. He would wonder about the past and think about the future, occasionally he would air out the motor and break the speed limit twice over. Sometimes he would glimpse Don in the rear view mirror, he never seemed surprised.

Once in a great while Gladys would ride in the passenger seat and they would head east in the morning, into the rising sun, on a long day trip in search of civilization and shopping and soft serve ice cream. Clyde really missed those sorts of days after she passed away.

Clyde kept the car parked in the lean to shed and fussed over the details from time to time. But Don had been a gifted mechanic even before death and he poured hours of his spirit life into every component, until it could never miss. Until it roared to life and hummed with a timing so fine it could only be supernatural. Every time Clyde turned the key the car was better; fluid, vital and eager. Now Clyde was buried in the Dismal cemetery and his car abandoned and forgotten. So every night, just before dawn, Don visited the car.

When he was satisfied he slammed the car hood down and moved through the driver's side door to sit behind the wheel. Spectral hands gripped the steering wheel longingly as in his mind's eye he saw the highway headed west and rested his boot lightly on the accelerator, his heart full of desire. His short brimmed felt cowboy hat was pulled low over his dark eyes, as he shut them he could see it all, he could feel the wind over the vast plains. He was free. As he opened his eyes, the suffocating inside of the shed door jarred him every time, the closeness of it was like the inside of a casket lid. The truth was Don was stuck. He touched the ignition lightly, the Hammonds had left the car with an empty gas tank.

The deepest dark comes right before the sunrise, and it found Don in front of the television in the living room of the abandoned house with the white siding falling off. He had his right boot resting on his left knee and his hat tipped low over his face as he leaned back in the recliner. He was a spirit, alone in the old empty house and he swiveled the recliner back and forth ever so slowly. He was getting tired and losing form. This was a flat screen model Clyde had brought home there toward the end and set in front of the old box television in the particle board entertainment center with the doilies on it. The remote was over by Clyde's recliner, Don didn't need it to turn the tv on and off. It was still connected to the rickety antenna on the roof and the local news channel filled with commercials would flit in and out between bouts of static. Don had never really taken up watching television but he had enjoyed the ritual when the couple had been alive. This recliner had been Gladys' last one, a hunter green velvet affair, short and squat with a swivel base and upholstered buttons in the back. The foam had turned hard under the fabric. Don clearly remembered the day the old couple had brought it home. Now he swiveled back and forth gently, bumping into shopping bags of knitting on one side and decaying cardboard boxes filled with vintage Reader's Digest magazines on the other.

When the sun finally rose in earnest Don was stretched out on the little bowed love seat with his boots up on one armrest and his head cradled on some decaying lace pillows on the other with his hat covering his face. His arms were folded tight across his chest and his ankles crossed, that was how he slept when he was tired. The pickup passing on the highway in the morning fog noticed that the lights were on in the old haunted house again.

2

Mermaids Never Drown

Mermaids never drown but Emmy was a woman with a secret.

Dallas, Texas
  March of 2025

Emmy started her morning by crying in the shower. Steam filled the room and shampoo bubbled and ran off the long pink tangles of her hair. Coffee brewed in the kitchen and the smell mingled with the oranges and mints and intertwining vanillas of her conditioner. Little rivers of hot water traced her contours and she cried the big, fat heavy tears that hurt so much to shed. She stayed the course of her inward chaos until it was time to be done crying. Then she directed her attention to the tile in front of her and her mind leapt to mermaids.

Those that knew Emmy best knew that she made something of a hobby out of crying. She cried in the beautiful mornings. She cried over cups of coffee and alone in her little car. She cried during happy times with loved ones and sitting in the sunshine with her plants and on nostalgic Christmas afternoons.

She cried on help-me weekdays, on save-me full moons and over old movies and new songs and new movies and old songs. She cried silently at night onto her pillowcase, saying to herself, I will take my own time thank you. She wasn't traumatized, facing any major life crises or clinically depressed at this time. (She had checked). She always just said that she was weepy and kept moving.

The tile in front of her was white with an iridescent flake, emotionally mesmerizing in a fish scale shape, she called the shape mermaid tile. Intricate, repeating on in simplified sameness, whimsical but full of weight, this project had turned out beautifully. This was the third shower surround she had designed since learning how to tile, if it would have been her house she would have done it in blue, not white. Shades of blue in colors so thick they would have left a haze in the air. Running her pointer finger around the grout grounded her. She cherished that fuzzy fingertip feeling. The patterns were falling together, overlapping, happening all over again and that spoke to Emmy's heart.

When the persistent internal separation threatened to exhaust her Emmy imagined mermaids. Mother of pearl and moonstone, turquoise and coral, sand on wet skin, the colors and textures always lifted her spirits. Mermaids were unrestrained, irreverent- uninterested in redemption. They plunged the depths of the ocean and never drowned in their own tears. No one asked mermaids dumb questions like, why is your hair green? Why have you collected so much treasure? Why do you stay in the coves and the inlets in the afternoon heat? Why do you go out to sea in the playful nights? People accept that mermaids do what they do because mermaids pull men down to their deaths if it suits them. Thinking about mermaids always cheered Emmy up. She firmly believed in choosing to be happy, every single day was a new sunrise waiting to embrace her.

When she stepped over her pile of discarded clothes she stopped to admire her purple pedicure against the striking black and white pattern beneath her feet. Emmy was in many ways a stereotypical millennial woman. Little lines were starting to form around her eyes where the skin creased when she smiled, life was just starting to get good.

By the time she poured her first cup of coffee her bubbly warm self was fully functioning. She eased out into the sun room to her computer desk and brought up Facebook on a worn out laptop with peeling Lisa Frank stickers stuck on the lid. Then she shut the lid abruptly and wheeled away into the profound solitary sunshine, oh to be irresponsible. Then she pull scooted herself slowly back in the desk chair and opened the lid again, borderline irresponsible yet refined, Emmy sat up straighter. What she wouldn't give to never open Facebook again, she felt technically trashed body and soul.

She longed to get into the passive zone like a blissful gradient slipping right into oblivion but that wouldn't set in for a few hours yet. Still– there was a sort of energy in this kind of passive creativity, like solar. Emmy continued to muse in circles to herself. The morning would be spent updating social media presences for a list of small businesses. This was a dull but steady task. Emmy pushed her over sized black glasses back up on the bridge of her nose and moved her coffee cup to the designated coaster. She used her sleeve to mop up the coffee ring it had left behind on Matt's desk. Some habits she couldn't seem to form.

Emmy took off her glasses and dialed her friend Phoebe's phone number from memory and got straight to the point.

"I have found, the best, blueberry muffins, they are so good and get this: they have no gluten, no eggs, no dairy, no nuts and no soy."

Emmy spread the wrapper out flat with one hand next to her coaster parked coffee cup, Phoebe sounded skeptical.

"What's in um then?"

"Probably cocaine. They are so good."

Emmy put the emphasis on the word so and Phoebe snorted in spite of herself. She had dreamed about the prairie last night and a daisy wallpaper repeat. Her friend Emmy continued.

"Are you ready for your big meeting?"

"I am so ready, I am really onto something this time. I had the most incredible dream, there were horses on a highway and all these colors of heat in the desert, it feels like a good story waiting to happen. I can't wait."

Emmy listened with her ear inclined to her phone, her friend's words were bringing to mind the sunglasses of the 1970's.

"Lady, you are going to be amazing. My mom loves you. You were born to do this. But are you ready?"

Phoebe loved Emmy for her optimism. That was what good friends were for, helping you reflect your intelligence back to yourself. Emmy smiled, still bare faced without her glasses, Phoebe was a seat of her pants sort of person and there was no way she was ready yet.

"Yes, I am ready. Actually, no. No. No I am really not. Actually maybe I better let you go. Love you!"

Emmy was ready for the good-bye, Phoebe had that kind of entirely directional existence, she was always in motion. So Emmy waved absentmindedly as if Phoebe could see her.

"Bye!"

Phoebe hung up without closing salutation, that was her custom in their friendship. Emmy followed up with a text loaded with twinkling stars, four leaf clovers, shooting stars and hearts, the happy kind of chaos. After the last colorful emoji circle she hit send with her index finger and a smile.

"Remember, you have lucky girl syndrome. You have so totally got this."

3

Nothing Is Ever Really Gone

In which Ashley makes a drop off.

Dallas, Texas
   March of 2025

From the cracked pavement in the parking lot to the smell of the aging air conditioning, the firing range was Ashley's favorite place to go when everything was shattering around her like an old windshield. She closed down the ride sharing app on her phone and headed in to say good morning to Frank. Ashley didn't drive.

"Good morning Frank."
   Frank offered the barest nod of acknowledgment. The range was deserted on a Tuesday, she spent most of her days alone but still Ashley craved privacy. This was her world, a place where she trusted herself. Adrenaline surged through her young frame as she proved her skill level to herself once again. Putting in the rounds felt purposeful and boosted her moral. She lived inside

virtual walls that she would never be able to break through but while she was here she almost believed that she had a chance. She had never fired her handgun anywhere besides the highly controlled environment of an indoor firing range. Thud. One more bullet buried, she tried to imagine a knee or a shoulder. When her day came they would take her anyway but hopefully it would cost them.

No one knew she came here except Frank the owner. She didn't think her mom or her sister Emmy would be surprised, in high school she had pursued motor cross and after that hiking and kayaking. They would say she liked to push her limits. Still, they didn't know that she frequented a firing range and they didn't know that her aqua college girl backpack had a concealed carry compartment. Most of Ashley's things were purely functional, all about just surviving the short term. Her mom and Emmy didn't know where she was, they were just another family hanging on to the fragments of being connected. Sometimes fragments are all that is left, her mom was never far from her mind.

Frank was reading a worn out newspaper when Ashley approached the counter. Someone was watching her from the strip mall across the way, waiting for her to leave. Ashley lived in a personal hell called the surveillance state. Frank jerked his head imperceptibly and shifted his eyes as he had done many times before. Ashley took a moment to watch from inside the darkened front windows.

"I know Frank, I know."

The old man nodded from his stool behind the counter. He watched her closely as she stepped out into the morning sunlight. Ashley was all about what you didn't see.

Frank spent his days watching people and wondering about people. Ashley looked like the college kids did these days, young in the face and like a genuinely nice individual. She was in survival mode but underneath that she had a bright generous smile.

She was a little old to be a college student but something about her said academia to him. She wore athletic shorts and sandals, like any college girl in Dallas. He guessed that she loved the rugged outdoors, something of the wild came into the range with her that reminded him of high mountain winds. She had a crystal stud in her nose. Frank had seen a lot of things in his day but Ashley was complex, nuanced and wide open at the same time. He could see that time was running out for her, whatever she was involved in was going to take her one way or the other. To Frank the gradual collapse from erosion and the coming loss of control was obvious. There was danger in isolation and for a woman like Ashley, there would be no safety anywhere. She might not die, she might just slip away without consequence. Frank turned his head minutely as she disappeared from sight. Then again, she might die.

Ashley was digging in the fridge when her mom emerged from the master suite in their high rise apartment on the Dallas skyline.

"Good morning sweetie. Big day today?"

Her mom used motorized black out shades and sleeping pills to start her morning whenever best suited her.

"Yep!"

Ashley spoke into the fridge, she was sure she had another yogurt in here somewhere. There was something she wanted to tell her mom but Barb was already at the door.
"Me too, see you tonight."

"Mom, wait a sec, do you want to have supper with me tonight? I could make-"

Barb interrupted her before she could finish.

"I'm sorry sweetie I have plans. Maybe next week?"

Ashley smiled.

"Sure, sounds good."

The apartment door shut behind Barb, handbag draped over her arm. Ashley gave up on the yogurt and headed into Emmy's old bedroom. How to love the emotionally unavailable had been one of her longer running side interests. There was too much static and interference. Ashley's darkest nightmare was that she would fail to intervene in time and her time was slipping away from her and she knew it. The illusion that she would always be there was just too comfortable.

As she stepped into her work space Ashley slid her feet into special slippers that she kept just inside the threshold and grabbed a pair of charge neutralizing wristbands from the side table. The room was lined walls, floor and ceiling in five specialized layers, partially to keep what was inside in but more importantly to keep her mom's frequency from messing up her equipment. All the layers felt claustrophobic to her but they were necessary so she endured, she wondered how she would cope with incarceration, formal or informal. For now this was her workspace. A series of sturdy folding tables around the perimeter of the room held a collection of home made technology and small mechanical tools.

Ashley plopped down in a low swivel chair and crossed her legs meditation style. On the table in front of her was what looked like a modified microwave with extra knobs on the front, she grabbed a clipboard and started twirling the dials as if she was cracking a safe, making notes with a pencil as she went. Pausing she slipped on a pair of clear safety glasses. When the door popped open she reached in with her bare hand and picked up the phone that was resting inside. The screen was shattered and clouded, full of jagged edges, the body was bent, Ashley knew it had suffered water damage. She smiled, everything left traces. Everything left traces. It was all just a matter of knowing how to look and that- was her life's work. Nothing was ever really gone.

From our thoughts to our spoken words to the trash we put in dumpsters, Ashley believed it all remained connected to us. She set the phone inside one last processing unit and contemplated her good luck charms while she waited. She kept them in a clear pouch out on the table, this was a good place in her countdown for a mini meditation. When she finished she took a thick triangular piece of metal out of the pouch and placed it in her backpack. It was an old sickle section, symmetrical but with so much rust and build up that it was no longer recognizable as sharp. Her mom had explained to her what it was when she was small. They had found it together in a wooden cigar box of childhood artifacts and Ashley had asked to keep it.

"You know, I asked my dad that a long time ago- and he said yes."

Ashley set the battered phone inside a foam lined black case and snapped the silver latch shut. Then she slid the case into the main compartment of her aqua backpack next to a similar but smaller black case. Ashley sighed, she was going to have to pick up a yogurt at the airport, getting too hungry on drop off days only made everything worse.

She was settled into a window seat before the nerves started. She turned to her go to coping method, trip planning. Usually after she made a big drop off Ashley took a vacation. Traveling was her hobby. She usually stuck with domestic and nature oriented trips and so her remaining to-be-explored list was dwindling. Trip planning just wasn't going to cut it today. She held her own hand in front of her rib cage comfortably. Ashley had been alone so long that she had difficulty recognizing that she was lonely.

Maybe she would take her sister Emmy with her this time. That would be wonderful, some sort of spontaneous sister bonding trip. Matt would throw one of his silent shit fits about impulsivity but Emmy would love the idea. Ashley opened her phone to start browsing for flights and hotels. Emmy would love a nice hotel, some place with a fancy lobby and really good beds for sleeping in in the morning. This was going to be fun. The woman next to her had a phone cover that looked like speckles on a bird egg, Emmy would love that. Ashley stared out the window into the clouds, speckled surfaces were like surface level happiness when underneath there is nothing, nothing at all. She was too tired to even overcompensate and still she continued on out of untamed obstinate instinct that functioned like a magnetic pull. Emmy would say fight, lift your head from the dirt one more time. If Emmy knew she would rush to her side and say fight.

Ashley was sitting on a bench in the Phoenix airport with a cup of black coffee and a new romance novel when David approached her and sat down. They sat together companionably for a moment. They had met this way many times and yet there was still a formality to be observed. He was a study in forced patience and timing. Ashley was brave because she had practiced bravery. He would always have the upper hand. She unzipped her backpack and placed both black cases into his larger waiting palm. His hands were pale and fleshy, specialized, like hers, but in worlds of different ways. David was as ethical as a corporate shroud and twice as smart. Ashley hated his hands.

She made the hand off without worrying about anyone seeing. There was nothing to be hidden, nothing illegal or illicit. She paid just as many taxes as anybody. She chose airports because they were public places, filled with cameras and people and because the extra trips blended into her frequent traveling habit. She had done everything she could think of to make herself feel comfortable with the drop offs, sometimes it was the little things that got her through. She lived under constant surveillance because David wasn't about to let anything happen to her, her skills were too valuable. So that only left the ramifications of her work, herself, David and the whole world and the eternity of the cosmos to be afraid of. If she was attacked for the information she carried maybe she would get lucky and be killed.

David regarded Ashley patiently, there was usually more to see if he waited. She was like the negative space in the desert. She was stressed but she held up under it beautifully. She was looking at the security cameras, her stress tells were like clockwork. Ashley's coffee was getting cold. She could never tell what all he knew.

"It's all here? A full recovery?"

Ashley scoffed, it had been a difficult project but she still took pride in her work.

"Nothing is ever really gone. It's all there."

The larger case contained the original phone that had been destroyed to hide evidence. The smaller case contained a drive with the information that Ashley had extracted. She sent both so that his analysts could compare and confirm her work. David echoed her sentiment thoughtfully.

"Nothing is ever really gone."

"You know what I mean, everything leaves traces."

"You know I have a different kind of project in mind."

"You know I could have handed this to the agent that followed me this morning and saved us both a trip."

"I enjoy meeting you."

Ashley didn't say anything or look at him so he continued.

"I believe you wanted to, "expand beyond hard drives to everyday objects and historical objects and possibly, eventually people." I could be the one to help you do that."

Ashley felt a new level of coldness as he quoted the careless words she had spoken as a college student. Words she had spoken to a professor, not to him. David could feel the animosity building so he eyed her weaponless backpack.

"So much time at the firing range, are you planning to shoot me?"

His voice was dripping with mockery then he straightened back up.

"So you need to think about taking on a more advanced project."

There was no question in his voice this time.

"That's not going to happen."

Ashley was surprised that her voice was level. David waited to respond.

"A lot of things could happen."

He could have put the emphasis on the word could but his tone was even, bordering on kind.

"I'll let you think about it before I ask again. These things are worth the time. You might need to mentally prepare, you have a major career change ahead of you."

The sinister power dynamics between them fell silent as Ashley saw broken triangular blades falling down, everything cascading apart everywhere around her. The world was out of timing, blades were chattering violently, what would blow apart next? What would she end up being responsible for?

She could not do this thing in front of her. Around her the shapes were clashing endlessly forever until the angst and the pain formed a sort of harmony called duty and destiny and change. Then her head cleared. Duty was a lie, she had never been interviewed, hired, inducted or trained. She had no mission, in a rush to use her abilities he had valued her skills above her as a person. Duty was a lie and destiny was not reality, tradition was reality. David could see the gears moving again. She was a remarkably down to earth tech genius. She would come to terms with what she had to do. She gulped some cold coffee before she spoke.

"Maybe the future isn't in front of us anymore. Maybe it's somewhere in our relics and memorabilia. Things change."
    "You've always made me proud. I'll be in touch."

With that David headed back to the private jet that had brought him to Phoenix, leaving Ashley sitting alone on the airport bench. He should have known not to trust anything you see.

4

Blue Horses

Barb doesn't dream.

Dallas, Texas
  March of 2025

For Barb dreams were like storm clouds building on a horizon that is out of sight. You still know they are there and wonder what is going to happen. She welcomed a new fight. Everything in her life had been firmly under her control long enough for boredom to creep in.

There were blue draft horses standing in the water in the corner of a fence line, in a hay field. Dark clouds overpowered the sky.
  She could see the finished stacks, imposing giants in the distance.

The horses stood still and time stopped. The barbed wire fence was half way under the water so that the horses sloshed as they milled together. Her dad was standing among them in the water, his hand on a very blue blue roan.

His straw hat was bent low over his face but she recognized his iconic silhouette, his posture, even the curve of the hat brim could only have been his.

"Dad-"

Barb never said goodbye before he died. The winds were picking up. She had abandoned him, made that final choice. She had let him go under the water. If only she would have grabbed him. Then he had gone where she could not reach him. The water was rising around her feet in the hay field.

"Dad!"

She called out like a small and frightened child.

He didn't seem to hear her. She was too late. She had been wrong.

Barb wanted to walk closer and make herself known but she couldn't move. She could feel the water rising around her legs.

The panic of claustrophobia washed over her the way it does in dreams. If he had known she was there, would he have acknowledged her? No one could count how many horses there were, maybe only three. Because they moved so much.

She was on an open grassland. She was part of the shooshing sounds of the tall prairie grass swaying in the wind. On the ridge above the little meadow pocket stood two figures, hand in hand. They didn't move and that scared her.

"Mom? Dad?"

Barb whispered hopefully as she walked in the grassland. Then she ran. A wall of wind came down against her and she struggled on.

"Mom? Dad?"

The figures didn't move. Didn't acknowledge her. They were just a photograph, like a mantel over a room they were perched on the ridge of the grassland.

"Mom? Dad? I'm sorry."

Barb fell down in the tall grass, the ground was wet, she was soaked. Would she be able to lift her head?

"I'm so sorry."

Barb whispered her painful secret even more quietly, hoping the photograph would hear her.

It was too late.

A single tear eased from Barb's left eye onto her pillowcase as she slept on.

Barb woke in the morning feeling tired but composed. She didn't remember the dream but she remembered that she had dreamed. She took sleep aids of natural and not-so-natural origins. She slept behind black out shades with the thermostat set to sixty-eight degrees. She even wore her heavy charms and talismans to bed. Whatever it was that had been pushing in on her, it was starting to break through her defenses. Maybe it was getting stronger, maybe she was wearing down. Maybe she was curious. Tonight she would try something different.

Her master suite in her high rise apartment was done in linen floral wallpaper and plush carpet that hushed away any sound from the outside world. Built in bookcases with recessed lighting housed her extensive collections of everything from seashells to Victorian songbooks. Tucked in a silver frame away in a corner place of honor, next to a piece of blue and white porcelain, resided a photograph of her parents.

The seating area in the corner featured custom upholstery and an antique reading lamp, a cashmere throw carefully folded and a television disguised as artwork. Barb loved to watch TV. The king sized bed was done in high end hotel like linens, and the headboard was white leather, a chic and modern note. Every decor choice was beautifully sophisticated. Barb was a curator.

Every morning that she woke up here she was overcome with gratitude. Of all the ways to wake up, of all the situations all over the world, here she was. She started her morning with her stretches, one and two and up to the sky above. She woke up her body by flexing her spine and all the tiny bones in her feet. She held her balance on the back of the reading chair while she flexed her toes and rotated one leg at at a time high and wide, like an aging ballerina warming up tenderly. Cat and cow and table and mesa and quick like a birdie, she moved through a sequence as personal as everything that surrounded her.

Her bathroom was tiled in blue marble with gold veining, reminiscent of Calcutta marble but with more sublimity. The vanity and ceiling were done in gorgeous raw oak, to keep it all grounded. This bathroom had been installed in the mid nineties but she had rejected the giant bathroom mirrors that were popular then. Instead she had gone with a series of three narrow and tall rectangular mirrors installed with panels of demure artwork in between them.
The chandeliers were handmade on an exotic beach from cut smoky glass and featured inlaid mother of pearl, they were done in long and narrow tiered shapes, as sexy as the sixties themselves. Barb found the soft glow they emitted reassuring.

Barb chose a tan linen pantsuit from her walk in closet, the sort of no-fail outfit that one reaches for when preoccupied with other things. Her wardrobe was filled with high quality fabrics and leathers and sensuous textures but remained surprisingly streamlined and practical. Barb had great taste, but you would find no luxury brand names here and certainly no stilettos.

Her jewelry collection however rivaled any boutique or jewelry store in the American southwest. The center of the custom walk in closet had been outfitted with rows of velvet lined drawers and glass topped cases. The cupboards and drawers around the edges were fireproof safes. She had been collecting for a long time, these were investment pieces. Some of them were very old. Many came from highly coveted artisans and exclusive names, many more featured unusual material pairings or craftsmanship techniques and even more pieces came with fascinating stories.

Most of them came from North America but not all of them. Barb had traveled widely and enhanced the value of the collection by placing pieces next to each other that most collectors would not have thought to. This was a collection that could impress any curator who had literally already seen it all. This master suite, this expansive closet, this was her sanctuary. No one else set foot in this space and no one had ever seen the true extent of her collection. Barb held her treasures quietly and kept her secrets closely.

She fixed her first cup of morning coffee at a little marble topped built in coffee bar outside her master suite bathroom. Her coffee reminded her of her dad, Barb tucked the red and black container away in the inlaid rosewood cupboard.

When she had finished applying her fake eyelashes she smiled at her reflection with satisfaction. Most people attributed her youthfulness to some form of witch doctor magic but really her secret was in her devotion to her skincare rituals and nutrition. From gua sha to tea to good old fashioned exfoliation and moisturizer, consistent effort was the real secret. In the past she had been surprised when people didn't believe her. Now she knew how little people believed in the power of consistency. She probably should have let her daughters see her rituals, her day in and day out discipline. How were they to know what went into her successes, if she never let them see? Barb sipped her coffee, they were grown, it was probably too late for that.

Before she stepped out of her sanctuary to start her day, Barb completed one final ritual, the most important one of all. The motorized shades were programmed to let just the barest amount of blazing Dallas sun into this corner of the suite at this time of day, the effect felt a little like early morning and a little like the shaded light reaching into an ancient temple in the jungle. On a handsome side table sat square trays filled with small pieces of hematite. These were black stones, shiny and rough cut, each smaller than a quarter, Barb preferred a mixture of tumbled and raw. Piece by piece Barb removed the jewelry that she had slept in, that she wore day and night. Piece by piece she looked them over carefully with a practiced eye in the perfect light, she was looking for cracks. She needed to know as soon as any of the pieces started to give, started to show damage. Next she set them down in the hematite to decompress. She expected the jewelry to eventually fail but she could prolong the lifespan of the pieces by using hematite to pull the stressful charges out of the jewelry.

Fully dressed but vulnerable without her amulets Barb rested her hands in midair above the trays with her eyes closed. Listening, feeling, observing and balancing the energetic exchanges taking place in the trays beneath her hands. When she was satisfied she finished her ritual with a series of closing chants and gestures.

When Barb had left home after high school she had not been able to leave everything, or everyone, behind her. That's when she sought out the education that a woman with a ghost problem needs, a little here and a little there. In the end that particular ghost had not been difficult to shake, once she knew how. The next problem had been the appearance of other ghosts. The paths were open, the ways were worn and she found herself vulnerable to picking up new visitors. Later on she had traveled the world, picking up new defense techniques as she went. These days nothing much bothered her.

Giving her talismans a few more moments to recharge in the sun warmed hematite Barb dropped handily to her knees on her plush carpet, to pray. The humility of the motion was at odds with everything else that made Barb the woman she was. She started with a long and formal Catholic prayer that completed her protective rituals for the morning.

Then she turned her thoughts to how good her life had been, how well things had turned out after the difficult start, all the things she was thankful for. This incredible apartment, this safe haven that had been her home for decades now. Her thriving business, her work that drove her and fulfilled her days. Her two daughters, the chance to have experienced the love of a family of her own, the women they had grown into. They were all healthy and safe. After everything early on that had made her who she was today, her daughters were whole and well. That was all that mattered.

When Barb stepped out of her master suite, which was really an apartment inside of an apartment, she left the vulnerable sides of herself locked up with her jewelry collection. No one need ever know that she had either one.

She would not think of her home or the past or her prayers again until she returned. She was a stunning professional woman that wanted for nothing. She was independent, fierce, laser focused. She was a boss, as the youth might have put it. And today she was meeting with Phoebe, a young artist that Barb knew had potential in spades. Phoebe would be her new rising star in the art world.

Barb felt goosebumps as she pushed the elevator button impatiently, she could not wait to see the work that Phoebe would be showing her today. The conversations, the connection, the exciting new energy a new collaboration could generate these were the thrills that kept Barb engaged in her work. Phoebe had everything that success would require and now she would have Barb to mentor her. Barb was the connection maker, the career builder, she called the shots and she was in control. She loved the way that felt and she was used to that feeling. Deep within her subconscious an uneasiness stirred, like blue horses standing in water.

"I am in control. I call the shots."

Barb nodded to herself as the elevator whisked her down to the Dallas heat and she put on her sunglasses to face the day. Today would prove to Barb exactly how wrong she was.

5

Phoebe Finds What She Is Looking For

Dallas, Texas
   March of 2025

Phoebe practiced astral projection and lucid dreaming techniques. She waved her hands fluidly in front of her face to cleanse her aura before starting her sleep countdown. The trance was broken by her grandparents calling in for a video chat.

"I'm good. I'm great actually."
   Phoebe tried to keep going with her breath work as she watched the clock in the bottom corner of the screen. Her grandparents were not convinced. She pulled her hair away from her face and around to one side of her neck in a characteristically introspective gesture. Her hair was long and done in elaborately imperfect curls. She looked like she might have worked in a popular salon.
Her grandparents weren't going to let it go.
   "No, it really is going good. I can't wait to call you and tell

you how well it went."

The muscles in her back were starting to tense up again. Phoebe felt them ebb and relax again as she smiled into the screen and waved her most adorable goodbyes.

"I love you both. Talk soon."

She was driving down a dirt road through majestic open grasslands. She drove slowly, looking at the colors. This was a warmly muted landscape full of open spaces and dynamic shadows.

Soft shades, browns with a lot of undertones, purples with a lot of haze, light murky blues with a lot of green, dark yellows and golds. These weren't the colors she was seeing but they were the colors she was feeling.

Lately she had been taking long walks and drinking more coffee than ever before in her life. Phoebe moved quickly, walked quickly. She was looking for inspiration, something worthy of a huge opportunity. She needed the income but she wanted to do this work from her heart.

This had to be something that she really wanted to explore and spend crazy numbers of obsessive hours on, not just anything would do. She needed something wild.

Now beads of sweat were forming on her forehead but she could not let go of the steering wheel. She was not in control as the car sped along a dirt path through the prairie and threw her side to side. This was a predestined journey.

This was the not a familiar dream pattern. This was something new, Phoebe could not believe her luck.

The car slid to a stop in front of a house. Phoebe's hand was cold on chrome. She couldn't get out, the door wouldn't open. She jerked harder but she remembered she was dreaming and stopped.

I'm dreaming. You are in a dream. She remembered all of her years of practice and tried to look around curiously. She could hear wind chimes, so interesting.

She could feel someone watching her. She saw a corral crammed full of blue horses, shoving against each other. She could hear their sharp whinnies. Someone was watching her. Water was rising all around the car. She tried the door handle again and made to crawl calmly across the bench seat to the passenger side–

This was a dream.

Where was the person who was watching her now? Were they friend or foe? She couldn't find them. Water was in the car now.

This might be a drowning dream. Phoebe hoped her decisions to become an interpreter wouldn't come back to haunt her.

A crow landed on the windshield with a heavy thump and splat of feathers, cawing, jarring Phoebe's ears painfully. She looked up at him and the scene dissolved.

Tall rust red grass swayed in the wind around her, she felt like a small child lost in an overgrown grassland. There was a ridge in the distance ahead of her and she struggled toward it through the grass.

Two people stood hand in hand on the ridge, looking down at her, judging her. She couldn't see their faces. They didn't move. She pushed on curiously. Were they real? Were they alive?

The sinister crow was circling above her, cawing. Blue horses were grazing all around her, paying no attention. She was coming to a barbed wire fence, there was a gap where the wires had gone slack. She could go through. Then she saw the puddle of water, she would have to wade out into it to cross the fence. She would do it.

Did she want to wake up? She felt at war with herself.

The daisies were turning to brilliant sunflowers. They were growing in a sunny yellow graveyard with pink head stones of all ages and shapes, some of these were very old. Phoebe thought this could have been a cemetery in Texas. The blue horses were grazing at random among the markers. They looked at her. She ventured on.

This was a dying dream.

Phoebe could hear a piano playing a hesitant melody full of missed steps and longing. She looked around, the piano needed to be tuned but the musician was skillful. There was an open empty grave in front of her but she only felt curious.

Should she stop? No, she needed to know.

There was a tombstone already in place over the open grave. What did that mean? She leaned in carefully to read the inscription but could not make it out.

Maybe this was a bad idea.

A crow was sitting on the flat top of the thick headstone, next to an old weather radio with bunny ear antennas. The crow hopped nearer. There was something shiny in it's beak that it wanted to show her. Phoebe took it in her hand, it was a driver's license. She would keep it. She would take it with her.

Phoebe was walking on the dirt road, the small card in her hand. Walking up the long driveway to the house. Barbed wire fences sagged on either side of her and the tall red grass rustled in the breeze. She could hear the car coming.

It was a loud, throaty car. She could see the headlights coming in the dark down an adjacent road. If the car turned down this driveway, she would be run down. The headlights panned as the car turned into the driveway. The car had no driver. Full of dread Phoebe noted that she had always wondered if this would happen to her someday.

Before she could run she saw a rock on the road. When she picked it up, another rock appeared a few feet in front of her, so she picked it up too. And another one appeared. The trail of rocks was leading her down the road to the house but she could still hear the approaching car. She couldn't look away from the trail of rocks but she could hear the car. And the piano. And the clanking graceless wind chimes.

Phoebe had fallen asleep on an acupuncture mat and when she woke with a start she howled in pain and rolled like a person on fire, reaching for her dream diary with a grin. This was totally unlike anything she had ever dreamed before. She had just hit pay dirt.

6

Matt Is Missing Something

In which Emmy makes a decision that will change the course of her life and the lives of her loved ones.

Dallas, Texas
   March of 2025

"Have you read this yet?"

Emmy leaned over in bed to look, it was the article about how to pose in honeymoon selfies. Matt had printed it out. He had one about looking your best in your wedding photos around here somewhere too. She had not read that one either. Matt had wedding planning materials spread out over the coverlet. He had taken his contacts out for the day and in his glasses she thought he looked like a super hero in disguise. She sat up to pretend to look at all the things he was looking at. He had invitation samples, sample caterer contracts, articles on what to ask for in floral arrangements, materials from photographers he was considering and more printer paper stapled in the corner about island resorts. Emmy caught his eye and held up the backs of her hands, wiggling her empty left hand ring finger humorously.

"I know! I know. I'm still working on what would be perfect."

Emmy let it go and looked at his color scheme selections for a while. She was a color buff and found some of his efforts amusing. Then she saw he had more wedding gown pictures so she put those away in his folder for him. He had even brought up her losing weight so as to fit into a smaller gown a few weeks ago. Sometimes Matt could get carried away with needing everything to look a certain way.

Emmy tried to read for a while but then rolled over to try to go to sleep. She was never going to be bridal enough for Matt's pictures. Her stomach was hurting about it all. They had been on again and off again for eight years. But she had still thought when the day came she would get an official proposal, of some kind. Her stomach felt heavy and turbulent all at the same time, there was another reason she couldn't marry Matt. She had been keeping a secret that would change everything about their relationship. Emmy's phone buzzed on the nightstand in their picture perfect bedroom.

An email from Cindy the realtor shattered the peace as soon as she saw it. Cindy needed the pictures for the house listing, Emmy took great pictures. Emmy looked around her in a panic. She had just declared this house, her Blue Mermaid house, her home, finished about a month ago. Matt was going to sell it.

She stared around wildly in a panic, three years of scraping up old linoleum, tiling floors and showers, pulling weeds, establishing perennials, painting trim, refurbishing cabinetry, pasting wallpaper. It was all slipping away from her. She had literally just tucked away all the swatch and sample boards she had made titled The Blue Mermaid House. This was a cozy bungalow with a wild cottage style garden for a backyard and just a hint of the ocean. Epic was what it was, this level of design work belonged in magazines.

Emmy waved her phone above her and thrashed in the sheets as she rolled over angrily.

"You said you weren't going to sell this house."

Matt started putting all his papers back in his folder and looked over his glasses.

"I said you had nothing to worry about right now."

"I want to stay here. I know the original plan was to sell this place but this could be our home. I love this house."

"You loved the last house and you will love the next one."

Emmy stared at him as rage built up. The first house, the one where she had learned to lay tile and design gardens, he had sold that one out from under her without telling her, without asking her. They had broken up over that. Matt had used the money to buy this house, the one that had become the Blue Mermaid House.

"I suppose you have a condo already picked out."

Matt missed the anger cues and smiled in a pleased sort of way before pulling a different folder out of his nightstand.

"Actually we are already in contract negotiations."

Plans for a new construction duplex were spread out where the wedding things had been. Matt worked the second jobs, saved every penny, a disciplined runner he never eased up or missed any details. He would be climbing the property ladder his entire life. Anger was turning into recklessness inside of her. Emmy silently wondered what the gorgeous Blue Mermaid House was worth now. He had done it all right. He would be selling her home. He didn't know it but Matt had finally pushed her over the line that she needed to cross.

"I don't want to see your pictures! I don't want to live in a condo."

Matt didn't take that moment to remind her that this house was held in his name and his name only. He didn't need to.

"You haven't even seen it yet. You'll love it. It'll be great."

Matt fully expected her to break up with him over the move. She got attached to places but they always got back together. He didn't expect what was about to happen next.

"Matt, I have something to tell you that I should have told you years ago."

Matt turned toward her mildly interested, Emmy was an open book. He couldn't even begin to guess what she might keep for a secret.

"You're already married?"

He joked, trying to get her to smile. He had known she would take the selling the house news hard.

"No. I own a ranch."

The pause was long.

"Like, a cattle ranch?"

"Yes. I own a ranch."

Matt's eyes narrowed the way she had known they would. There were several reasons she had never told her boyfriend when she inherited her grandfather's ranch.

"In Texas?"

"No, in Nebraska."

He eased into a comfortable smirk.

"Like a hobby farm sort of thing."

Emmy didn't like that statement. This conversation was going nowhere good anyway. It was all going to go downhill from here.

"No."

Emmy let her answer hang in the quiet. Matt had worked several steps ahead of her and was already back around to the guilt attack.

"Why didn't you tell me?"

Emmy could have said, because you like thinking of me as dependent on you. Or because you would have pressured me to sell it or do this or that or the other thing with it or because you wouldn't be able to stand that I have accidentally already won the property ownership race that is so important to you. Instead she said something very honest.

"I didn't want to."

II

Part Two

7

Everywhere You Go There You Are

Dallas, Texas
  March of 2025

Barb's linen trousers fell to a precise hem point on her leather shoes with the stacked wooden heel. This had been her first gallery and she still swelled with pride every time she walked up to the front door.

Barb Donahue sold art to private collectors and investors, oil tycoons, finance and stock market clients, international buyers and the occasional museum. She was exquisitely informed on what was and wasn't available on the market. Barb knew the clients- and she knew the artists. More importantly Barb knew how to put the two together in a way that created lucrative transactions. Beyond that she knew how to build artist careers that made sure those investment pieces held and increased in value. She had opened her first gallery here in Dallas and now she owned a second gallery in Santa Fe and a third in Phoenix. Barb's eyes never wavered and her step never faltered. She had never been an artist but she had always been a curator.

Her appointment today was already waiting for her in the private showroom in the back. Barb's entire emotional range included: a high point of mildly pleased, a neutral resting zone of peacefully grateful and an all time low of mildly aggravated. Today she was quickly accelerating from neutrally grateful to mildly pleased. She had sniffed Phoebe out as a grad student and she expected her upcoming collection of work to be the one that Barb had been waiting for.

When Barb arrived in a flurry of handbag and sunglasses and shook her hand firmly, in a flash Phoebe saw herself the way the older woman saw her. It wasn't just her artwork that Barb was interested in. She was herself, an investment piece. But not in an unkind or uncaring way. They were about to undertake a sort of journey together. Working with Barb was going to change the trajectory of her life.

Barb regarded Phoebe with a keen eagle eye. Phoebe was a Korean-American woman that had spent her childhood summers in France. She possessed a certain combination of qualities that made her presence and her vision flat out addictive. Powerfully restrained inner charisma balanced with a very American unrestrained enthusiasm. Barb saw that unrestrained enthusiasm in a lot of the women in their thirties, her daughter Emmy for example. But in Phoebe it just worked, her outward mannerisms were sophisticated. She was irreverent but soft. Phoebe was a one in a million woman with a unique artistic vision. The portfolio had not even been unzipped yet and Barb was already mildly pleased. She sipped her coffee in anticipation.

Phoebe was sweating. Last time she had been in this room she had forgotten to inhale at the proper time and gone into a coughing fit. She wished was was back in her car, accelerating away from here. Why hadn't she just taken a job as a community college art professor years ago?

"So."

Barb leaned forward.

"Tell me about the sketches for this collection."

Phoebe could feel the excitement radiating from Barb out into the air. Phoebe wondered how old Barb was, the older woman had this zeal for life and a healthy glow that made it hard to tell.

"Well- um, you are aware of my previous work depicting dreams?"

The statement turned into a question at the end as Phoebe grasped the portfolio zipper.

Barb waited silently.

"I was inspired by a very specific dream that visited me. It was a narrative experience and I have enjoyed documenting and depicting that."

Barb hadn't blinked. Phoebe was starting to feel dizzy as she prayed silently. Please let her like it. Please, please let Barb like this work. Then Phoebe slid the first drawing from the portfolio.

The impact was like dropping an emotional bomb. Time slowed around them. Barb's eyes narrowed and Phoebe could hear Barb's heartbeat change pace. Phoebe turned wide eyes toward Barb and jumped. Barb wasn't looking at the drawing. Phoebe could hear her own heartbeat thundering in her ears. Barb was staring at her, right into her miserable little soul.

They locked eyes for an awkwardly long microsecond and Barb seemed to relax a little.

"Phoebe- dear, you are sure, this is a place you saw, in a dream?"

Phoebe didn't understand the question right away. Her big beautiful eyes searched the upper right corner of their vision limit and back and forth of the floor before answering quickly.

"Um, yes. I am sure."

What was going on here?

"Hmmmmm."

Barb pursed her lips.

"And I believe you are interested in the subjects of the sub-conscious mind, dreams, and the connections there-in?"

The right corner of Phoebe's lip pulled downward as she hung on Barb's every word. Please let me sound smart she prayed.

"Yes. I spend a lot of time in those areas."

Phoebe replied, feeling slowly for every word.

"And I imagine you spent a lot of time, when planning this collection, pondering what I would like to see? Would want to see?"

Phoebe wanted to bolt from the room and never come back but now she was curious. "Um. I- suppose I did."

Barb was drinking her coffee again.

"Well. I am impressed. That- is a drawing of my childhood home."

Moments passed like millenniums for Phoebe. What had she done? What could she possibly say? Should she apologize? Was this a massive invasion of privacy? But it didn't look like Barb expected her to say anything.

"Don't worry, I don't suspect you of any kind of snooping."

There was a smug look on Barb's face that dared Phoebe to ask why. Phoebe had never resisted a dare in her life.

"Why not?"

Barb smiled darkly.

"Because that's not what it actually physically looks like."

Phoebe hadn't slept well in days and hadn't eaten any breakfast, there was just so much hanging on this meeting. Now she was vaguely aware of a stylish gallery assistant pressing a hot cup of coffee into her hand. Barb was nowhere to be seen. Her portfolio was gone.

Oh my GOD. She had spent way too much time and energy thinking about what Barb would want to see. What had she done? What had she gotten herself into? Looking into other people's anything without permission was highly unethical. What would Barb think of her practices now?

And Barb was not the kind of woman that one trespasses on. Phoebe would never have glanced into her office without being specifically invited, much less her mind. Oh my GOD. Phoebe wondered if the sales girl had a brown paper bag and the patience to help her hyperventilate into it. She didn't even really want to be here in Barb's private workspace much less snooping around inside her inner world. She was scrambling for her phone. Her foot was already mashing into the accelerator out there in the parking lot. Then Barb was back, the portfolio nowhere to be seen.

"I am VERY impressed with your work- and with you."

Barb slid back into her seat and continued.

"I thought it might be best if I took a quick browse. You have been wandering around in my dreams– and it's hard to tell what you might have– come across. What might come up."

Phoebe stared uncomfortably and waited. Her usually disciplined posture had evaporated into a heavy and resigned weight in a plastic chair. Her spine was starting to cramp up, her rear was going numb. She was going to be crippled by the time she got out of here.

"Tell me Phoebe. Do you believe in ghosts?"

At that moment Phoebe was wishing she could just become one.

Community college art professor, community college art professor, a quiet life as a community college art professor, she chanted inside her head. How could this day go any farther off track?

"I do, yes, I guess I do."

Phoebe was reaching for competency. Barb seemed to be contemplating her next cup of coffee.

"Hmmmm."

The awkward silence stretched on.

Phoebe finally had something to say.

"I am so sorry for invading your privacy, I never meant to–"

Barb cut her off.

"To be fair to you, I should tell you that I suppress my dreams. I have known for a while now that messages have been trying to come to me through my dreams, and I have chosen to block them. I do not think you are at fault because they found another way to reach me."

"I had extremely high hopes for this collection and for your career."

Barb continued bluntly.

"And now I have even higher hopes."

Phoebe again had nothing to say.

"But it is going to take me a few days to process this ability of yours, to look at the work. To think about positioning. Can I call you toward the end of the week?"

And just like that Phoebe found herself out in the hot Dallas air and abandoning dignity she ran in her high heels to her car.

8

Fifty Plants And Dead Cats

Dallas, Texas
  March of 2025

Emmy wandered into the kitchen and stopped at the coffee bar to fill a beat up green thermos and shut off her basic Mr. Coffee brewer. Everything visible in this home belonged to Matt. She eyed the rows of matching coffee cups displayed on the open shelves. Her rag tag collection was stored in the cupboard underneath with her mom's old thermos and her red plastic tub of grounds.

The mermaid tile didn't sparkle in the sun when Emmy packed her toothpaste collection. The bed had never been that comfortable, her clothes had always looked a little shabby in the custom closet. Emmy had left Matt many times over the years, this time was going to be different. She was thankful as she packed that her natural hoarding tendencies had been kept in check by Matt's relentlessness. All of it was going to fit in her car, except the plants. There were more than twenty orchids alone. The sun room was a veritable jungle where she sat at her computer like some kind of exotic queen holding court among the leaves. Plant lady was the new cat lady after all. A girl could bring home as many plants to as she wants to fill the void. And no one cares if you stuff fifty of them in one room and a few of them die. Matt could keep the plants, he would need them to finish showing or selling the house, or whatever he was doing, in magazine worthy style. He could have the the fifty dead cats for all she cared. The orchids would probably die where she was going anyway. Her phone buzzed.

A text from her mom's work number read.

"Can you finish up with Sophie today? I saw what you sent over, needs more polish."

Emmy cracked her neck sideways in stress and inhaled deeply before texting back.

"Authenticity is king these days, I think she's fine."

Emmy wanted to walk away but her phone pinged again.

"We are the finest dealers in the business. Do it over."

Angry tears traced their way down Emmy's freckled face. She was so mad at Matt.

"So much concern over how things look. How about a little more concern for how things actually are? Sophie is great, the content we have put together is true to her work and true to her as a personality, call her and find out."

Emmy hit send with an angry jab. Then tapped out one last word on the matter.

"I am not redoing it."

Then she erased that message and typed a new one instead.

"I will look it over for more polish and it will be done today."

Hypothetical conversations swirled in Emmy's head. She was

caught somewhere between employee and business partner. She had other clients but her mom was by far the most time intensive. Handling the social media presences for Barb's personal brand, the online presence for her three galleries in separate and distinct communities and building the individual brands for the artists Barb worked with, without it all mushing together and having the same voice- was an enormous storytelling undertaking. She would love to never ever open Instagram again. Emmy went to find a B vitamin. The phone buzzed again, another text. This time from Matt.

"Pasta sound good for tonight?"

Now she couldn't procrastinate any longer. Emmy put her small collection of crystals and rocks into her laptop bag. Then she gathered a few loose photos and sticky notes, a really good eraser, a clothespin, a frayed cord to some device from 2010 and some old hard candy from her desk drawer. The clutter was a Matt deterrent. It all looked vaguely sticky. Then she took out a manila envelope.

The envelope was worn, the letter inside even more so, from all the unfolding and folding through the years. The handwriting featured light strokes of exaggerated cursive with left handed idiosyncrasies here and there. Sometimes she opened the letter just to look at her grandfather's penmanship, it was something remarkable from another time and place.

Dear Emmy,

We do not know each other well but I have thought of you often. I am leaving the ranch to you instead of to your mother. I wish it to remain in our family and I know that she would sell it. I have left the ranch solely to you however it is my wish that you share the lease payments with Ashley. I know you would have done so regardless. I hope the money blesses both of your long and happy lives. I have left your mother a separate sum of my life savings. I have also left several boxes of your Grandma's things to Ashley specifically.

Please accept my highest regards,
  –Clyde

Reading his handwriting was like meeting him in person. She was loved. Ashley was loved. They were provided for by an unseen distant angel of sorts. He had gifted her with stability when she had needed it most. He trusted her. Family. The word always jolted her. The ranch was to remain in the family, her family.

9

Empty Houses Fall Down

Dallas, Texas
   March of 2025

Now she was holding a piece of paper with a home phone number and a cell phone number scrawled in left handed cursive. She decided to dial the cell phone number first. She leased her ranch to one Mr. Hammond, a cattle rancher. This had been arranged by her grandfather. Emmy had never spoken to him but twice a year he deposited a lease payment into a local bank account in her name. Her grandfather had planned the transition very well, all the details had been ironed out ahead of time. When Emmy first realized the amounts of money involved she enlisted Ashley to help her. Now Emmy felt confident everything was in order.

"Hello?"
   A deep and brusque voice answered on the second ring.
   "Mr. Hammond, this is Emmy Donahue."
   She was acutely aware of how feminine her voice sounded on

the line. Then she thought she could actually hear him stand up straighter and give his full attention.

"Good morning. What can I do for you?"

His voice struck her as genuine and kind.

"Well, this is going to sound a little bit odd but- I am wondering about the house. The house there at the ranch."

Emmy pursed her lips together and then took the dive.

"I am thinking of coming to live there for a while."

"Uh, oh, well, um."

He sounded like a man in his sixties or seventies, grasping for both thoughts and words.

"Let me see here. We shut off the water. The power is still connected. No one has been there for several years. You- you know that? The house really isn't in that good of shape."

Emmy had expected reasons not to do what she intended to do and was ready to take it all in stride. She nodded her head.

"I could imagine that. Do you think it is redeemable? It doesn't make sense to me to own a house and have it just rot and fall down."

Mr. Hammond could tell in that moment that he was going to like Emmy Donahue.

"Yes. I think it could probably be turned around. Like I said the water needs turned on. The power should be good to go. I think the roof is still holding good, so there shouldn't be that kind of damage yet. I would expect there to be mice but all the windows were intact last I knew. Yes. I think it could be turned around."

"I'm glad to hear that. I'm thinking of coming tomorrow."

Mr. Hammond was a gruff but basically kind older man with four adult sons, one daughter in college and one daughter in high school. The kinds of ideas that came from young people did not register much surprise with him anymore. He was puzzled to hear from Ms. Donahue but not displeased. His gaze was fixed on the horizon behind his sunglasses as he adjusted his plans for the day to include a run over there to turn on the water.

"Well I can certainly run over there today and get it unlocked and get the water going, look it over a little bit. Do you know how to find it?"

And so their conversation continued. Emmy found that Mr. Hammond repeated himself a lot but she could tell he was used to doing business over the phone. Toward the end of their phone conversation something else occurred to James Hammond.

"Emmy you need to really think about what houses are like when no one has cleaned them out. I mean, Nora and I went over and cleaned out the fridge and later we went back and did the freezers– but that's it. All your grandpa's things are right where he left them. Actually all your grandma's things are right there too. He never moved them or did anything with all that when she passed away."

Emmy listened intently as Mr. Hammond paused.

"I just want you to know what to expect."

10

All The Cards

Dallas, Texas
  March of 2025

Barb went back to her gallery later in the day, as planned. Her mind was roiling in pretend conversations and complex potential scenarios and she was mumbling to herself. She had taken enough ibuprofen to bring down a horse but the tension pain in the front of her head was still there. She wasn't feeling well at all and that bothered her.

When she grabbed the heavy front door of her gallery she heard someone say her name in the distance behind her. More than a little annoyed she pivoted– and there he was.

Allan was better looking than she remembered. His energy field felt like a refined oak writing desk that had been weathered by the wind and sun on the beach. Sturdy and trustworthy with elegant lines and comfortably worn out and rapidly losing color. He was a lanky man wearing a denim jacket that he had worn for thirty years, even in the springtime Dallas sun. He chilled easily. She loved how the seams of the jacket made clean lines from his shoulders to his hips, Barb felt a little something stir in her stomach.

"You have entirely too much time on your hands."

Allan had been sitting on a bench under a tree near the gallery entrance, waiting for her.

"Well- you don't answer your phone or return my messages. So, you know."

He had strolled close enough for Barb to see his eyes behind his rimless bifocals. Allan gave Barb pause in a world where almost nothing did.

Against her will Barb asked the question she knew he was waiting for.

"Fair enough. What is new in your life?"

"I am officially retired, for real this time. I've been up at the cabin for the last six weeks or so. The fishing has been phenomenal. But I miss you."

Allan had always been a man that got straight to the point in conversation. He wanted to waste her time.

Barb's thoughts must have shown on her face.

"Have you caught many fish?"

Allan was momentarily stumped.

"Well- no. But my portfolio is full again."

Allan drew architectural sketches in pencil that Barb could pour over for hours. She saw him in her mind's eye, sitting by the waterfall sketching, fishing pole forgotten. His artwork and his mind was a fascinating place. So was his fishing cabin in the mountains and his bedroom, if she admitted it to herself. Allan had known Barb a long time and he could tell he was starting to crack the armor.

"You remember the waterfall? The campfires we made there on that rock?"

Barb had known Allan for a long time and he was always one to put his cards on the table too quickly, thank God he hadn't been in business. But still, their on again and off again relationship was one of the bright spots in her life, like patches of sunlight. She was starting to realize she had been missing him too.

"Come in, I have a new collection of sketches in the back. You are going to want to see this."

Barb carefully arranged Phoebe's collection on the carpeted work table. She was starting to appreciate Allan's arrival as serendipity, she needed help to look at these pictures. She needed to find out what they meant. Barb didn't dream. She made sure of that. Memories resurfaced in dreams. Messages and connections and desires emerged in dreams. Barb was mildly impressed with herself and with Phoebe. She had blocked out her dreaming so thoroughly that her dreams had made their way to her through a different person. Barb raised her eyebrows and angled her head as she thought about it. Allan was watching her closely.

"What is going on with this collection? You seem impressed."

There was also intimidation and fear and anger and grief and rage but he stuck to impressed.

Barb had dated Allan off and on through some of the best and worst times of her life, as a single pregnant woman, as a single mom and when she had that bout with recurring flu that seemed to last a year and a half. It was a tribute to their comfort level that she didn't mind being seen like this in the back room of her gallery. Barb never let anyone see her vulnerable, not her daughters or her friends.

"This reminds me of where I grew up."

She gestured to the first picture, the one Phoebe had shown her. Allan stepped forward to look at it more closely.

Barb gestured to the next, an abstract of two people in a landscape with a house behind them in the distance.

"This reminds me of my parents. Weird, huh?"

Barb's voice had become very sad.

"Barb, everything about you is weird. I mean, you have a high incidence of very unusual phenomenon."

"Yes I'm aware of what goes on around me. That doesn't worry me. This feels different. How could Phoebe paint my dreams?"

As Barb questioned aloud she shifted to agree with Allan. Weird yes but in her everyday world certainly not that weird. Phoebe had picked up on a wavelength that contained Barb's dreams, unnerving but not problematic. Maybe she was over reacting.

The power flickered off and then came back on and Allan glanced at Barb sideways.

"Do you think you can start to calm down now?"

"I do actually, thank you for your help. I'm glad you were here."

Allan beamed and seemed to swell with joy and Barb smelled trouble.

"Barb I'd like you to come stay with me this weekend. Or next weekend? I want to show you the new things I've been working on, no pressure, no big deal just a good time with a dear friend."

He reached out and took her hand.

"At your cabin in the mountains?"

Barb would never admit it but she loved it there, it was serene and safe and clean and well designed. Her face showed none of that sentiment.

"Or we could go somewhere else? We could take a quick trip? Where would you like to go?"

"Allan- I can't go anywhere right now. I can't come to your cabin this weekend or next weekend or anytime soon. I am so busy with the galleries and my girls. I'm just really happy with my life right now and I have so many things to do."

The lanky man in the denim jacket with the brilliant eyes nodded his head and took her hands and Barb felt compelled to say more.

"Why do you always come back to me? I've never taken time for you."

"I guess I have always hoped that someday you might want something more stable. We are aging you know?"

Then he put all his cards on the table.

"Barb, I love you. I have always loved you. You know that. Please let me in your life."

Barb was beginning to passionately hate this stupid day.

"I know you love me Allan. And I love you too- in my own way. I understand what you are trying to say. Maybe we could take a trip together, I'm just way too busy this month. My calendar is packed, I need to go over to the Santa Fe gallery this weekend."

She hugged him far longer than she should have and she could feel him relent.

"Okay. I'll call you. Answer your phone, okay?"

He hugged her tight, his heart skipping every third beat and his throat constricting, he loved her more than words and missed her terribly.

11

Have You Ever Been To A Ranch

Dallas, Texas
  March of 2025

"How did it go?"

"Your mom is freaking weird but I think I'm down for that."

"Well good luck."

Emmy and Phoebe were ready for their shift to start at Today's Cup, a popular local coffee shop owned by an old family friend.

Emmy was feeling very tired but she was happy her friend's meeting had gone well.

Later on in the rush Emmy asked again.

"Well, I don't know, it was just kind of weird. Like we had a lot more in common than I realized. Some things surprised me. This might be a lot more than I realized I was getting into."

"I get that. She's a complicated person for sure."

Phoebe thought that was the least of it but she had decided not to tell Emmy about dreaming someone else's dreams and making artwork about someone else's dead parents and childhood home. She would probably tell her later, she just needed time to process.

Phoebe had desperately wanted to become clairvoyant and now that it looked like she was getting what she wanted, she felt the need to keep it to herself. She just needed to talk to her family. Later in the coffee shop chaos Phoebe decided not to tell her grandparents either. She would just wait. Maybe this would turn out to be a good thing for her. Maybe no community college art professor gig after all. Whatever Barb had in store for her, she would reach out her hand and take it. Right now she just wanted to curl up with a good book and forget the whole thing. Simone the owner had taken a shift at her third location across town, when she arrived back Emmy was immersed in explaining to Phoebe how one showers with orchids.

"I know it sounds a little odd and personal but they really do well with the heat and the steam. So I just set them on the edge of the tub and then I take them out of their pots, you know one at a time and I just hold it under the water with me."
Phoebe had one penciled eyebrow raised.

"Well you know, they don't actually have roots. The part in the pot looks exactly the same as the branches above because they grow on like cliffs near waterfalls, they don't really need dirt. Their roots are just wrapped around like a little bit of moss or peat or something. And it's so cool because they like take the water in and their green vein things sort of like swell up with the water and expand and grow while you are holding them. Right there in your hand."

Emmy had not realized how wrong that was going to sound

until she got to the last few words and and then she started to smirk and continued on without apology.

Phoebe snorted and broke down in giggles that led to the big stress relieving laughs. Oh my gosh she was stressed. She had needed a laugh like this all day. Emmy loved to make people laugh more than anything and listening to Phoebe made her laugh even harder. Soon she was smacking Phoebe on the back while trying to save what was left of her own eye makeup.

Simone was a seasoned business woman in an uncertain labor market and when Barb had offered up these two as short notice substitute baristas Simone had accepted gratefully. It had turned out to be a small but effective part of holding it all together week by week. Now Emmy was trying to fix Phoebe's eye makeup with a paper towel but she couldn't see through her own tears of laughter and they had both started laughing again. The shop wasn't busy right now. In moments like these Simone wondered who was actually helping out whom. Their laughter was just too contagious though and Simone started to smile, who cared.

Emmy spoke up again.
  "No, seriously. I have an actual question for the two of you."
  Phoebe and Simone looked at each other sideways.
  "I don't know, I don't know much about plants."
  Simone quipped slyly.
  "No, seriously, have either of you ever been to a ranch?"
  Emmy's tone was enthusiastic and exacting, as if this had been the topic of conversation all along.

"You mean, like where your mom grew up?"

Simone was Barb's oldest and dearest friend.

"Yes, that's exactly what I mean. Where I mean. Have you ever been there?"

Simone was shaking her head no thoughtfully.

"I have been close to your mom since you were a baby. I don't think she has been back to where she grew up at all. And I know that she is, sensitive– about her parents."

Simone paused and then continued.

"What have you got on your mind?"

Simone, with her ebony skin and real warmth and full range of emotions was her mom's opposite in every single way. And Emmy loved working in her coffee shop and just being around her. Even though Simone was clearly already unimpressed, her first move was to ask for more information. She loved Simone so much.

"Did you know that when my grandpa passed away he left his ranch to me? Not my Mom."

Emmy explained with a note of tenderness in her voice.

Simone was processing emotions at a rate that exceeded the speed limit and the corresponding facial expressions flashed across her face. She opened her mouth and then closed it again.

"I did not, know that."

She paused again.

"That has been a few years ago."

Emmy nodded in agreement.

"Yes, that's exactly it. Well the ranch has a house on it, an empty house. And I'm thinking of going to live there."

Simone rubbed her temple, she needed to get this place closed down. She was going to be up late tonight trying to process all of this. Phoebe had been taking it all in with a very odd expression on her face. Now she was staring at her friend as if she was only just now meeting her. Life with Emmy was never boring.

"You, own a ranch?"

She managed to make the words "a ranch" sound as prestigious as British royalty.

"Does your sister know about this? What does her sister say about all of this?"

"Well she knows about part of it, I'm meeting her when I get done here."

"Does this mean you are breaking up with Matt? I saw your car is packed. Are you coming to stay with me?"

"Could I? I'm leaving for the ranch tomorrow morning. And yes, I am leaving him."

"I have never figured out what you see in him."

Emmy glared at Phoebe in faux outrage and then laughed.

"Well- he is very good at some things."

Simone raised an amused eyebrow and the two of them stifled their snorts of laughter and got down to scrubbing. Apart from being a comedy side show, they were actually very good at cleaning. God knows she needed all of that she could get. Closing time was coming. Simone decided to retreat to the pile of paperwork in the back that she had been avoiding. What was her dearest friend going to do with all of this?

12

The Mustang And The Malibu

Dallas, Texas
  March of 2025

Ashley was waiting for Emmy and Phoebe when they reached the parking lot that evening. Phoebe excused herself and disappeared in a roar of acceleration and sub woofers. The mini disco ball hanging from the rear view mirror threw specks of light over Phoebe's tired face as she waved a flirty goodbye to the sisters. Emmy mellowed into the deep vibrations, for Phoebe the year would always be 2006. Phoebe loved her white Ford Mustang GT with a passion usually only found between middle aged men and minimum value sports cars. Hopefully she would get a good night's sleep tonight, Emmy knew how tired working with her mom could make a person.

Ashley jumped forward and Emmy hugged her back, rocking back and forth and attempting to lift her off the ground with a giggle. Ashley hugs were rare. Underneath the playfulness Emmy could sense a deep darkness.

"Oh I love your hugs."

Emmy rocked harder. When were things ever going to be better for her little sister?

"Did you finish a job?"

"I did."

Ashley spoke softly in a self satisfied sort of way.

"One of the most challenging of my career so far."

Emmy smiled at her. Her own eyes were aching with emotion as concern pounded in her chest. What was wrong?

"I am so proud of you! We need to celebrate tonight. Get in, let's go eat."

Ashley crawled into the mess of personal items piled high in the passenger seat without hesitating or complaining or commenting. Maybe Emmy was leaving Matt for good this time. Emmy turned the car toward the main intersection and continued.

"You are positively glowing, did you get paid?"

Emmy took her eyes off the road and stole a glance at her little sister.

"Did you get paid a lot?"

Ashley smirked slightly in response.

"You did! You did."

"Six figures."

Emmy accidentally braked and barely missed hitting her nose on the steering wheel.

"From one job?"

Ashley smiled and laughed.

"Do you want to go on a trip with me? To celebrate? I was thinking hiking or maybe surfing."

Emmy would be hiking nowhere but she nodded happily.

"Sure."

Emmy didn't seem to notice the facial expressions of the other drivers as they wove around her. She never did. Her car shuttered violently as it crept along in crowded lanes of evening traffic and dark exhaust bellowed from the tailpipe. Ashley brought up car shopping every chance she got but tonight she didn't mention it. Emmy could afford a better car. She just didn't want a better car. The sun was setting. Ashley settled back in the seat and leaned her head closer to Emmy, thankful just to be together. They would either reach their destination eventually or the car would die it's last death en route. Either outcome was fine with Ashley tonight.

Later that evening found the sisters in a Chinese restaurant under a glowing red lantern.

"Are you sure what you do is, safe?"

Emmy blurted it out. Even though they had been down this conversational road many times before, she wanted to be reassured. Her tear ducts were getting achy.

"Well my pay it totally on the books and documented. I only take the jobs I want."

That part was not true and Ashley knew that on some level Emmy could sense it.

"I stay in public places. And really all I do is specialized tech repair. Like a fancy computer repair shop."

Emmy was nodding and replied without even a suggestion of sarcasm.

"Yeah. Mmmmhmmm."

Ashley sighed while Emmy waited in faux absentmindedness,

she had all night.

"Okay yes I am, very specialized. I have developed my own techniques and very few specialists-"

Ashley dropped her voice to a whisper.

"Okay, no one, right now can do what I can do. Or hope to do."

To Emmy that last part sounded full of regret but she decided not to push it.

"That's why so much money?"

Ashley nodded, her mind seemed far away.

"Do you need to do this forever? Don't people like you, like, retire?"

Ashley privately wished that was the case. The ambient music played on around them.

Emmy helped herself to another wonton.

"Well I have some news myself."

Emmy began tentatively, Ashley gave her her undivided attention as she took a bite of lo mein with a fork.

"I'm moving to the ranch."

Ashley appeared not to have heard her.

"Well, I'm thinking of moving, actually I've been thinking about it for a long time. I know it sounds crazy but I really think it could be a good thing for me. It doesn't make any sense to own a house that I can't get rid of and can't rent out and then just let it fall down. Empty houses fall down."

Ashley cut her off and held up her palm.

"I agree."

"You do?"

"I do. You've been needing to make some changes for a while now."

"I know."

Emmy continued after a few bites in silence.

"Maybe I would like it there. And you know it bothers me, having income that I don't know a thing about. I'd like to see it."

Ashley was waiting patiently and also visualizing her favorite beaches on a slideshow in her mind. Emmy continued on.

"I just don't know. What is mom going to say? What do you think? Should I do it?"

Ashley focused on her beloved older sister, sitting in front of her in the glow of red lanterns.

"Well my biggest question is, what are you going to do about Matt?"

Matt and Emmy had broken up and gotten back together so many times Ashley had lost track.

"Leave him. I've got to leave him for real this time, he's planning a wedding."

Ashley sipped her water.

"I think you're on the right track. Did you tell him?"

"No, I just packed up and now I'm here."

"That's kind of crappy but he deserves it– so fair enough."

Ashley had never cut Matt any slack.

"Back to your earlier question, Mom."

They sat in silence in the hustle and bustle around them. Emmy started.

"I think I have to tell her."

Ashley agreed. Then she asked the big question.

"Has she ever told you why she thinks you have to sell it?"

"No. She just gets super-angry-emotional."

The two sisters sat in silence in the crowded restaurant glow before Emmy continued.

"Kind of hysterical. She just says things like, it's haunted, it's not safe, our family needs to get rid of it, I need to stop being so selfish and listen to her. She can be pretty brutal. I haven't brought it up in a long time."

A tear was starting to ooze in the corner of Emmy's eye but she flicked it away quickly. Ashley remembered it all very well. She often found herself in a mediator role between her mom and sister. They were so different and so alike. They were both super strong personalities but they navigated the world differently. They could barely plan a lunch together. Much less resolve a long standing family conflict.

"I just need a little bit more to go on. Like getting hysterical isn't enough to help me make such a big decision. I'm more than willing to listen to her try to explain. I'd like to work through this together somehow."

Ashley cut in.

"She won't explain. She doesn't think like that."

"I know. She just expects me to obey her wishes, and then goes into name calling. She must be really traumatized about something. I don't want to upset her with this move. But she's going to be so upset."

Emmy pressed her fingers into her forehead.

"But I'm also an adult here. I can't just not do this because she won't like it."

Ashley was starting to see her vacation evaporating in front of her. The more she thought about it the more she saw what a Pandora's box Emmy was opening here. Yet she still stood by her initial reaction, this was exactly what her older sister needed to do with her life.

"You're right about that. This is a good move for you. You need to do it."

Ashley was blocking off time in her mental calendar to act as an on call therapist for both of them and it showed on her face. Emmy noticed.

"What are you thinking about now?"

"Nothing, just thinking maybe I should take some time off, like you were saying. I have a few personal projects I could work on. Develop some new skills."

The city lights pulsed and the traffic lights flowed around them where they sat and the moon moved across the sky above them.

Ashley leaned back in the red vinyl booth under the red lantern. How many more nights like this would there be for her?

13

What You Are Looking For

Dallas, Texas
   March of 2025

Matt was the extraordinarily hot guy in the grocery store line.
His t-shirt draped off of his shoulders and over his chiseled
arms in the ideal form of the male model. He was frequently
the hot guy turning heads in the grocery store line because he
was frequently at the grocery store. Tonight he was making fish
and a green salad and the penne with white sauce that Emmy
loved so much. His thoughts turned to his girlfriend. He could
not get over her and that bothered him. The check out girl was
hitting on him, he turned to the transaction at hand.

"Cooking for my girlfriend, she loves pasta."

The check out girl was wondering why none of the losers she
had ever dated had ever cooked her meals.

Matt was putting his groceries carefully on the floor behind the
driver's seat of his SUV when he realized he hadn't heard from
Emmy.

"Thinking of you. How was work?"

He put together a text with a lot of emojis then he took them back out.

Emmy loved to go overboard with emojis. In the last few years he had started sending her a lot of emojis back, it made her happy. They had reached a kind of softening like that.

On the way back to his house in the suburbs he went through a car wash and checked his phone while the the windshield was covered in suds. Still nothing back.

He parked in the attached garage and stopped to sweep up a little dirt with the broom and dustpan he kept on a pegboard in the front of the garage. The garage floor was shiny and reflective, getting it epoxied had been a wonderful decision. He had his eye on the market and this house was going to be perfect for a young family. The area was developing exactly as he had thought it would when he bought the place. His eyes fell on the shiny reflective floor in the empty space where Emmy's little car was missing.

Dinner was ready and waiting in the oven when Matt stepped into the shower. That was when he knew she had packed up. He got back out to look in her closet, her clothes were gone. Her nightstand was empty. Wrapped in a towel he leaned out into the sun porch and flipped on the light, her desk with all the orchids was cleared, except for the orchids.

He was not actually that upset. Years ago this kind of thing had gotten under his skin and irritated him to a frenzy but after all the breaking up they had always gotten back together again. He felt he was aging and mellowing out just a little. She was going to have a hard time with the move. He could expect another freak out before the wedding and probably one after. He turned the oven down and took a long shower in peace.

"Hey. I made you supper. Would you please come home? I want to hear your side of this. I love you and we can figure this out."

Matt rolled over on the couch, he had tried to game but Emmy had always gotten to him. He couldn't ignore it. There was no one as wild as Emmy. His phone buzzed with an incoming text.

"I'm moving to my ranch in Nebraska."

No emojis- she was one of a kind but so incredibly difficult.

Matt had to sit up and think for a while.

"I know you're upset but can we talk about this? Have you already left?"

His phone rang.

"I can't marry you."

Matt was not at all surprised or devastated to hear her say that.

"I know I haven't proposed. I know you want a ring. I promise it's going to be everything you have ever wanted."

He could hear her heart softening a little, he could make good on that promise. Emmy was an easy person to know very well.

"It's not just that. I'm ready to move to Nebraska. I need to go see it for myself. So- I'm doing that. It's what I want."

Matt let the long pause feel respectful and quiet.

"I hope you find what you are looking for. Will you come home for one more night? Before you leave. I will really miss you."

14

Not Home Anyway

Dallas, Texas
   March of 2025

The next morning the Malibu was parked back in it's designated spot in the spotless garage. Matt had left for a morning run and Emmy had one more difficult conversation to get through before she could finally get on the road.

Barb was seated at the expansive island in her high rise kitchen. This was the scene of so much of Emmy's childhood. She got a hard lump in her throat. In some ways she wanted to go home to her mom's love and approval but here she was in her mid-thirties. The time for that was gone. Her mom usually wasn't home anyway, on any level.

"Mom, I have something really difficult to tell you."
   Barb leaned forward and adjusted her large black framed glasses to get a better focus on her laptop screen.
   "I am planning to move to the ranch."

Barb fixed her with a deadpan stare so vicious that any gladiator or samurai would have retreated. She adjusted her glasses again for extra emphasis.

"Emmy, you listen to me. I have something to say about how you have handled this entire thing."

Every word coming from her mom's mouth was more vehement than the one before it. Tears were already starting to pour down Emmy's face, why had she even put on makeup this morning?

Barb was gathering her thoughts to find a starting point and when she leaned forward again and blinked- the power flickered and went out in her high rise apartment building. The connection was lost on Emmy's phone and she never got to find out what her mom had to say about how she had handled the entire thing.

"That went better than I could have hoped for."

Emmy whispered to herself and her coffee go cup. Then she shut off her cell phone and put her car in drive. As she drove through the sunshine she dried her tears.

15

Sticky Notes

Dallas, Texas
  March of 2025

Ashley was laying in bed staring at her alarm clock in the morning sunshine, just enjoying the silence. Her bed was a sea of white fluffiness. Her blonde hair was tucked behind her ear as she rubbed her cheek gently against her pillowcase. The alarm clock display disappeared when the apartment building's power went out. Ashley rolled over onto her back and stared at the ceiling. That would be it then, Emmy told their mom about the move.

Ashley felt bad for the building's owner and the contractors that had built it, no one would ever be able to figure out why this building had so much electrical trouble. The electrical contractor hadn't done anything wrong. Almost against her will her mind shifted to the that eternally repressed question, what was the deal with her mom anyway?

Ashley had spent her young life pioneering in technology. She was used to having no one to turn to, having no one who could answer her questions. She grabbed a sticky note and a pen. Sometimes writing her questions down helped her see them in a new light.

Why is mom's body radioactive?
   And what are the implications?

For her life span?
   For her health as she begins to age?

There was more than one reason Ashley lived at home. It wasn't likely that either Emmy or her mom would ever fully appreciate the situation.

What happened to mom?
   What was the source?

Ashley stared at her row of six sticky notes. She was used to having to problem solve all alone. Still she was aware that assuming she always had to be alone could become a bad habit. She really needed to talk to someone, this was probably the most important thing to be pursuing. Ashley was trying desperately to forget about David and she knew it wasn't going to work.

That afternoon Ashley opened the apartment door to a courier. This was how David sent her things, everyone was used to the deliveries. This had been how her very first project had arrived against her will, years ago. Ashley took the envelope, just a flat legal envelope not a package. The courier was an agent that showed no expression. Ashley's heart felt dead as she took it to her office to open, probably just a very small chip that he wanted data extracted from. Her mom had left in a mood, presumably for the gallery.

There was no tech in the envelope. These were faux news items, drafts. Ashley understood the idea instantly. Then she forced herself to look. These had been rough years, she told herself she was tough. The first one was about a gallery in Santa Fe being vandalized. Ashley had never thought about such a thing, really she had expected more from David. The second one was the draft of an obituary for a woman named Emmy Donahue that committed suicide. Ashley felt herself go into numb capability as she held the paper.

She would have that son of a bitch if it was the last thing she accomplished in this life. The third draft was her own missing person report with one of her own sticky notes with David's cramped handwriting on it.

"Start developing your tech. I will be in touch in six months."

III

Part Three

16

Desert Journey

Santa Fe, New Mexico
  March of 2025

Sophie's work in the Santa Fe gallery was even better than Emmy had expected. Sophie worked in pressed flowers and the imagery they inspired. Emmy held one finger to her lips and the other arm across her body as she walked along from piece to piece, standing still and moving her eyes.

"I'm going to Nebraska."

The gallery manager had the most interesting purple nail polish.

"It's been good to see you, you should come over here more often Emmy."

The manager waved goodbye to her as she made the door chimes ring.

"Thanks for all your help."

Leaving the gallery Emmy saw herself reflected in a shop window, her image superimposed over gobs of priceless turquoise

97

and a selection of Native figurines, rabbits and horses and coyotes. Instead, with a stab in her heart, she saw her mom, and her sister. They had been so blessed to spend so much time here together. The street and sidewalk ahead of her made a path underneath the crisp spring sky.

When she headed North and left the city behind her Emmy gunned the accelerator in the Malibu just a little.

"Let the good times roll."

Twenty minutes later she was pulled over along the road, squatting down low to take some scenic pictures at the appropriate angle. Back in the Malibu she studied the images and sipped her coffee, time was getting away from her. She put her little shaking car back on the road. Then she saw a set of buildings with the most fantastic coloring and she sighed and pulled over abruptly. People in New Mexico drove so slowly that no one minded. Shaking her head to clear her mind Emmy took another set of pictures. Would she ever make it to Nebraska if she stopped to look at every single thing that she wanted to look at in New Mexico? She still had all of Colorado ahead of her.

Back in the car Emmy turned up her music and turned back into the sporadic traffic. This was her adventure, she would go at her own pace. Hours and days be damned. She was pulled over looking at sagebrush when she wondered if God above was watching her from that distant blue sky. He would probably understand.

That day on the road Emmy took more than six hundred pictures on her phone. Beautiful bright spring weather shone down on her and she soaked it up. She drove slowly and listened to music. Who knew what kind of a woman she could grow into in a new state? Maybe she would even become an honest to goodness cowgirl. Emmy smiled to herself, Phoebe would love that.

That night she stayed in an aging hotel situated on the edge of town in the sagebrush. She was washing her hair when she realized that she hadn't cried since she left Dallas. She wanted to jump out of the water and call Ashley right then but she refrained. She was on the right track.

The desert vistas stretched to the heavens cradled around her. Places like these could make anything feel epic. Emmy grasped the steering wheel tightly as she felt so very alone in the solitude, there was no point romanticizing sadness. That sort of thing was almost as useless as glamorizing mental health problems. She had had enough of all of that for a lifetime, all that was left to do now was be happy.

As she shuddered down the desert highways Emmy never wondered if she would make it. The wide open sky stretched for miles above her and the sun baked spring earth basked for miles around. Instead she wondered if her mom had ever taken this road. She wondered if the artist Sophie could capture the colors and shapes she was seeing. She tried to decide if she liked urban living or being the only soul on the face of the earth better. She thought about hawks and how good their vision was and if she would see a snake at the roadside stop and why she had never taken up wearing turquoise jewelry. She wondered about being the darling of the desert or the queen of the range and imagined bands of wild horses.

At an isolated junction of two tragic deserted highways some-where in mid Colorado anxiety started to set in. This was no place to have a break down. She hadn't gotten lost in the desert but now she felt she had lost her way. Maybe taking her time had been a little foolish. She felt she had already used up her last chance to turn back. Emmy pulled over and took Clyde's letter out of her bag to read it again. Family. Trust. A connection from the past to her future, she could do this. Then she got back on the road.

Finally she laid her head down at a hotel in north eastern Colorado, in a town that smelled funny and her enthusiasm started to pick up again. Tomorrow she would see Nebraska.

17

Emmy Arrives

The Heartless Ranch, Nebraska
March of 2025

She stopped to consult the screenshots she had taken from various apps and Emmy felt confident she would arrive without confusion. Cell phone service had become sketchy at best. The highway was ever more deserted and beautiful, Emmy sighed happily. She loved to drive. She would know she had the right place for sure because the old mailbox by the highway would say Donahue on it, though she might have to look closely.

She had to be getting close. The Malibu puttered down a long flat stretch of worn out highway, she could see a mailbox coming up on her right. This was it, the Malibu eased to a stop. Emmy got out and peered at the mailbox closely. She had to bend over because the mailbox post was broken and the actual box was hanging upside down but there it was, her name, Donahue.

She took the time to stretch and look around her more carefully.

The landscape was deserted, no people, no cars and no other houses. She felt it was just her alone with God and she felt okay with that. The ground felt alive beneath her feet as she got back into her car. This was her land. So she turned her little car right at the mailbox and drove slowly down a dirt path lane. Grass had grown up in between the track and close on either side of the road. She could hear it brushing against the bottom of her car. No one had been driving here.

She followed the trail to a group of trees. An old tire was hanging on a fence post in the fence line, "NO HUNTING" had been spray painted on it in white paint. A little further along she saw another tire, this one said "BEWARE" – but it didn't say of what. She tried not to let the sign bother her, she had been psyching up for this, for years really. She drove around a corner to the left and pulled into a large clear space in between a smattering of buildings. She parked her car in front of a house with falling down picket fence. She simply couldn't look at everything fast enough. She wanted to see it all, know it all, take it all in immediately. This was surely the most interesting and exciting moment of her life. What was her place like?

The house in front of her was white, basic and low slung, tucked beneath some large trees. There was a jagged little cement walkway up to the front of it, and some picket fence around the front of the house mixed with some metal and wire fencing. The front gate was open. Emmy's heart panged as she missed her mom. This was where her mom grew up. Walking up this little sidewalk? As a little girl? As a teenager? The emotions were flooding too fast. She wished her mom was there with her so that she could hold her hand and see it all from her point of view. Emmy got out of the car. Her mom wouldn't have held her hand even if she had been here.

18

Welcome Home

The Heartless Ranch, Nebraska
   March of 2025

The sidewalk led up to a thick and generous cement step, old dead weeds and the new growth of spring crowded around it.

There were three red bricks propping the door shut. There were two doors, the shredded remains of a screen door and an interior door with a glass window. A window frame to the right sagged beneath a window air conditioner. Emmy could see now that some of the siding was falling off the house, this was extra wide 70's style siding. Here and there she could see the decayed original clapboard showing through, it was white too. This had always been a white house.

A cool breeze sent Emmy back to her car for a jacket. With a start she remembered she needed to let someone know she had arrived.
   "Thank God."

Emmy whispered when she saw the little bars on her phone, she had service. That was odd but very lucky. She sat back down in her car and dialed Ashley's number from memory and Ashley answered part way through the first ring.

"Did you make it? Are you there?"

"Um yes I am here, yes!"

"WELL- put me on video I want to see."

Urgency rang in her sister's voice.

"Slower, slower, oh my gosh."

Emmy walked back up the sidewalk with her phone in her hand out in front of her, acting as a tour guide.

"Okay, yes."

Ashley declared, apparently satisfied with her video inspection of the front of the house.

"What else have you seen so far?"

"Nothing, I just got here."

Emmy replied patiently.

"Well I'm glad you called, let's do this thing."

Emmy jumped and looked behind her for a loud banging metallic noise and spotted a windmill in the yard. The breeze was picking up into wind. Broken wind chimes rang near the front door. She hadn't noticed those before.

Emmy set down the phone while she zipped up her jacket properly and then virtually together the sisters did a slow 360 degree pivot. Ashley noticed and questioned everything that Emmy didn't.

"What are those small buildings? Where does that dirt trail go? What is that? And what is that over there?"

Ashley wanted to know everything.

Most of her questions would go unanswered. At long last

they commenced up the sidewalk and stepped onto the front step. Emmy turned to take in the view of the yard from the slightly elevated height. Late afternoon was starting to turn into evening.

She laughed nervously as she tried to move the bricks with her foot and then had to bend over and move them more deliberately. The screen door protested, wobbled and threatened to just fall off the house onto her but the solid door opened easily.
"Mr. Hammond must have come over and left it unlocked for you."
Ashley observed.
"Ashley, do you have time for all of this?"
Emmy just realized how long they had been on video chat.
"Of course I do."
Ashley didn't need to add duh to the end of that statement.
"What about mom? Is she home?"
"Nope, she said not to expect her until late."

The darkness and the smell seemed to pour out of the open doorway over her. Musty stagnant air, some sort of a soapy smell and notes of decay and filth. Emmy needed a moment but Ashley urged her on. She felt for a light switch and the kitchen lay before her. It felt very odd, different than she expected, very-colorful. The light bulb revealed blue, lots of blues, red, orange, yellow, strange greens it all seemed to compress together. She was feeling a little nauseous.

There was so much to look at, from the ceramic owl canisters by the sink to the bread box with the horse on it to the lace covered and the crocheted, it was a whirlwind of texture and motif.

And dust, grime and caked on cooking grease and dirt. The flooring crackled as Emmy walked on it, the glue underneath the linoleum was coming loose. The floor was a very busy orange and yellow pattern. There was an overflowing hat rack to her left, coats and cowboy hats were jammed and layered until the thing had to take up a five foot circumference. The floor in front of the door was littered with old cowboy boots and newspapers. Emmy noted one pair with spurs still attached. There was a flashlight hanging on a nail on the door frame and a set of skeleton keys. The sisters were totally silent for a long time.

They veered right through an arched doorway into a living room with two decaying and decrepit recliners. There was a box TV in a stand with decorative kitsch items all over it. Emmy swallowed painfully when she saw that one recliner still had a crocheted blanket thrown over the arm, where it had last fallen when the occupant got up. This might be enough for right now.

They peered into the bedroom off the kitchen and into the bathroom that also opened off the kitchen. There were two more small bedrooms and a sort of utility room on the back of the house. That was all there was. Emmy shut the front door firmly behind her and propped the screen door shut with the bricks and strode purposefully down the steps and the crooked front walk to her car.

"Emmy."

Ashley's voice was heralding her attention from inside her phone screen.

"Where are you going to stay the night?"

Ashley's voice was a little too direct. Her sister was really worried. The sun was really setting now and she couldn't see much on the video chat screen.

"Right here in my car, you've heard of camping right?"

Before Ashley could protest Emmy continued on boldly.

"There is no one around and I'll lock the doors. I'll be perfectly safe. And in the morning I will see this place with fresh eyes."

At first Ashley's only answer was a doubtful silence then she replied conversationally.

"Well I guess I can stay up with you on the phone, I didn't exactly have plans for the evening."

Emmy was secretly thrilled to hear that and a little sad when her sister was distracted.

"I'm expecting mom soon, why don't I call you back in like an hour and a half?"

"Sure."

Emmy was watching a glowing spring moon rise in her rear view mirror.

19

What Happened Over There Anyway

The Hammond Ranch, Nebraska
   March of 2025

Mr. James Hammond had his mind on the roping on TV in the den instead of the supper in the kitchen or all the family around him. Most of their suppers these days were eaten on the go, or perched at the island. Or in his case, in his recliner in the den. His wife Nora was setting garlic bread on the table. Tonight their grown children were home and the house was filled with horseplay and laughter. Their youngest daughter Zoe was a junior in high school this year and she was fully engaged in an argument with her older brother Zeke. James couldn't make out what they were arguing about. Beth was trying to help her mom with the food and telling August about her introduction to literature class. Beth was in her first year of college at the university. Only their two oldest sons were absent tonight. Jake lived in Wyoming with his wife and their new baby. Brian lived on the north end of the Hammond ranch, he was married with two children and one on the way. If they would have come over that would have meant putting the extra leaf in the table.

At long last the table was set and the sun had gone down. The darkness wound tightly around the patio light outside and pressed against the dining room windows. The Hammond ranch house was a mid century modern done in brick with large windows with sweeping views of the meadow that stretched out in front of the house to the sunset.

Zoe was deep in discussion about prom dresses. Zeke was barbing her about vanity. Nora was wondering who all would be helping with the post prom party this year and if Beth wanted to come home from college and help out. At big family suppers everyone talked at once.

"Did you go over to the Donahue place today?"

August leaned over to ask him.

"Yep-"

His father took a bite of garlic bread.

"Went over there to turn the water on, that pump is just about done in I'm afraid."

All the family members around the table stopped to look at their dad.

"Why did you turn the water on?"

Zeke asked blankly.

"Well Ms. Emmy Donahue called me this morning. And she asked me too."

They all stared quietly at him. He continued eating as if he didn't notice.

"Why would she call about the water?"

Zoe was a quick and inquisitive girl.

"I imagine she is going to want to use it, she is coming to live here."

Mr. James Hammond took note of all his family's emotional reactions. His son August on his right looked deeply troubled and thoughtful worry lines etched his face. August was starting to age a little, his engagement had fallen through and he was having trouble moving past it.

His younger son Zeke was already talking animatedly to Zoe.
"I wouldn't stay the night there for a million dollars..."
"Yes, you would..."
"Yeah you're right actually I would."

Beth had her head tilted to the right, pondering. She was wondering what kind of an individual their land lady was anyway. James suddenly locked in on his wife's face, she had been looking at him for a while now.
Nora was sitting down but she didn't need to stand up to make a point.
"You should be more concerned about her. Does she under-stand that it is haunted?"

Nora put the emphasis on the word haunted.
"Well what do you want me to do dear?"
Mr. James Hammond had been married twice and raised four sons and two daughters and was actually even older than he looked. He knew better than anyone that people will do exactly what they intend to do. He was thinking about his recliner in the living room.

"James?"

Nora persisted.

"Hmmmm?"

"When is she getting here?"

"Oh, um, she said today would be her first day."

All heads at the table turned to look out the patio door windows speculatively into the night.

"Do you think she is over there right now?"

Beth sounded scandalized and concerned.

Nora's heart was bumping nervously in her chest. What had her husband done now? He didn't always see things the way everyone else did. She looked at her son August. Maybe they should get in the pickup and go over there yet this evening.

August looked back at her briefly, he had been wondering that too.

"Should we go over there? James, what if she gets hurt?"

"Hmmm."

James was helping himself to more spaghetti.

"James! We know that place is haunted. You know it well enough to accommodate it. And this young lady does not know. That puts us in a situation of responsibility. And liability."

She added the liability as an after thought, oh my goodness she was getting tired.

"She won't get hurt."

Five faces turned to look at him again.

"How do you know that for sure Dad?"

Beth's voice was still laced with concern.

"I never got hurt did I?"

James was starting to get tired.

His family contemplated this silently. He had been hit by lightening while riding horseback and survived. On two separate occasions. The horse had been killed both times. He had been in horse wrecks, rolled his pickup once and had that heart incident. Each individual was lost in their own thoughts about whether their dad had ever gotten hurt or not but Zoe had always been the most focused family member, in her own way.

"But Dad you didn't ever live there, did you? Or stay the night there? What is going on with that place anyway? Why is it haunted?"

James was about ten minutes from just taking his plate to the den but he made one final effort.

"That's her family home over there. Everyone has to face who and what they are eventually. If you live to be as old as I am you will figure that out. She won't get hurt because in all these years and there has been a lot go on, no one has ever been actually physically hurt because it was haunted. So I figure that she knows her own business."

His family listened a little sheepishly. He added.
"She has our phone number."

"But Dad, do you know why it is haunted? What happened over there?"

Zoe persisted and looked to her mom for reinforcement.

"Your dad knows the whole thing, he was there."

Nora chimed in helpfully. She had never heard the whole story herself.

"I was young. Maybe six or seven."

"But Grandma Doris was there."

Nora wouldn't let it go.

"Well if Grandma was there, Grandpa was probably there, didn't they talk about it?" Beth was such a tender soul and it rang in her voice.

"They did not. Some things are better left alone."

James spoke over his shoulder as he moved to the den, already looking for the TV remote.

"But what about the car?"

Zeke was a young welder with more energy than intellect.

"Yeah, didn't a car go missing?"

Zoe felt a little left out, she was so much younger than her siblings that many of the old stories were news to her. August was the oldest sibling at the table and had yet to say one word.

"Explain to the kids why we can't keep tractors or vehicles over there. And then we will leave you alone."

Nora had found the remote and was adjusting the volume for James.

James was tilted way back in his recliner with his eyes closed. He spoke back to the kitchen in an absent minded tone of voice.

"He was a mechanic. He loved cars."

He spoke as if that explained everything.

"He was a bronc rider too."

James added as an after thought.

"Who? Who was he?"

August finally offered up a question from where he was scooping ice cream into various bowls over by the microwave.

James was watching the TV with his eyes closed.

"His name was Don. Don Donahue."

Nora was getting excited about the mystery of it all and finally getting some answers about all this.

"You mean Clyde. His name was Don Donahue and those closest to him called him Clyde. We leased ground from him for years. But- Clyde only passed away a few years ago. And that place has been haunted since you were a kid..."

Her voice slowed down and trailed off.

Zoe and Zeke looked at each other. Zeke would be driving out early in the morning. Beth wouldn't be too far behind him, going back to school. August had a house in town where he parked his cattle truck. Tomorrow night this place would be back to normal- James in his recliner. Nora in the kitchen and Zoe coming home after track practice and fussing over her goat tying and her goat herd, eating enough for three teenagers and falling asleep in a heap. Beth was thinking maybe she would come home again next weekend. Yes, she definitely would.

20

Emmy Spends Her First Night

The Heartless Ranch, Nebraska
   March of 2025

Emmy sat in the dark- alone in her car in the middle of nowhere
and she reflected that she was doing better with it than she
might have thought. She dug a pillow and blanket out of the
back, plugged in her phone, locked her doors and closed her
eyes. They popped back open again shortly but she kept trying.
The moon was unusually bright and cast the front seat in a
patch of moonlight. The wind had picked up even more. This
was a very windy place. Shadows careened around her in the
darkness outside her car. When Emmy broke down and checked
her phone it wasn't even ten yet. She jumped when she heard a
crow.

"Crawwww."

"Okay. Okay- my goodness."

Ashley texted several times to check on her, then she decided
to game for a while.

And now it was 10:30. Emmy pictured her younger sister in her room in the high rise apartment where they had grown up. Ashley had minimalist tastes that focused on serenity. Her bed was low to the ground with a floating profile and a sleek driftwood like headboard. Emmy spent some time remembering the trip the three of them had taken in Arizona when Ashley had met the artisan that made that bed for her. Traveling with their mom when she was in her curator state of mind had made for some fantastic experiences. They were lucky, very lucky to have a mom like their mom. The memories made her feel warm.

It was colder out on this spring night than she had counted on. This was scary but still not as scary as she had expected it to be. She wondered if Ashley would be calling her again soon. Emmy peered in the rear view mirror at the pile of possessions stuffed to the ceiling in the back of her car and over at the passenger seat. It was dark but she knew exactly what she had. A very colorful and odd assortment of ragtag items. Eclectic was the nice word for it. She laid her cheek back on her pillowcase. It was a flannel pillowcase in red and white plaid, leftover from an after Christmas sale. Reaching her arm around to dig further into the backseat without hurting her neck she found the bear Matt gave her last Valentine's Day and yanked him out into the front. He was a pink bear holding a red heart that said "I love you" in pink glitter on it, only the love was just a heart. Emmy squeezed him tight to her chest and rested her chin on his pink fluffy head between his pink ears. She already missed them all. What had she gotten herself into? Was it too late to just go back to Dallas? Everything was wrong in Dallas. Emmy didn't know what coming to Nebraska was going to solve but that's how life

117

had always done her, maybe she had been too reckless.

Once again she took Clyde's letter out but instead of reading it she just held it in her hand and closed her eyes. He had trusted her enough to leave the family property in her care. She was going to have to trust him in return.

21

No Point Staying Mad

The Heartless Ranch, Nebraska
  March of 2025

The ghost had spent the day wandering slowly in the grassy foothills, soaking in the sun. He rarely got tired of watching sunlight. One could drink it in and never get enough.

The sun had already set when he made it back to the ranch yard, he was a little behind schedule tonight. When he came around the edge of the house he stopped suddenly and squinted, his lips slightly parted. Right there in front of the picket fence was a strange car, with a girl in it.

The light from her phone was casting an eerie glow on her face. He wondered if she would see him. He wondered if she could see him. He wondered if he wanted her to see him. Then he retreated to gather his thoughts.

Who could this be? Shouldn't she be getting back on the road soon? He leaned gingerly out around the edge of the house for another look. A Texas license plate. A girl in her thirties. He stared hard at her face and a palatable thrill of recognition shook his vapor form to the bone. She looked just like Clyde. The square face. The strong jaw and the chiseled cheek bones. Hot damn, they were back in business. He was so fascinated he forgot to duck back behind the house. He had to see more, know more, figure this out. She was gripping a pink teddy bear and the glow from the phone was gone, the moonlight was reflecting off the windshield and the hood of the car. He held very still and thought for a while, he didn't want to scare her away. How could he get a better look?

The ghost had forgotten all about the cellar door and the nightly walk and the windmill and the front step. He had even forgotten about the shed and the car. He felt so alive. Eager and excited the spirit absolutely hummed with intensity.

Presently he knew what to do. Sometimes he could grab things and other times not. Sometimes he could open doors, or car hoods and sometimes he just went through them and into the guts of the car. He rarely needed to but sometimes he could travel by thinking of where he wanted to be, by disappearing and reappearing. He decided to try it tonight. He reappeared right next to Emmy's passenger side window and stayed perfectly still.

Maybe she would be able to see him? He leaned over slightly so he could see in the car. She had her eyes tight shut and her face smushed against the bear on the driver's side door, like she was determined not to look. She was clutching an envelope tightly in her right hand. The ghost had no heart but his heartbeat accelerated out of control as the girl opened her eyes and turned her head and looked right at him. And through him at the ranch yard, she couldn't see him at all.

The pounding sensation throughout his being eased off, she would not be alarmed if she could not see him. So he watched her carefully until she fell asleep. She could tell she was being watched but she was writing it off as being watched by an animal like an owl or as being nervous spending the night in her car in a strange place.

What was she doing spending the night in her car in a strange place? What did she think she was she doing here? She was reckless, that much was obvious. She probably made lots of stupid and dangerous decisions. Don the ghost could ask for nothing more than a friend full of bad ideas. This girl was going to need his help. The thrill of pure joy lit up the ghost's eyes. All of his loneliness was forgotten, this young person right here was going to need help.

He had all night, so he walked around the car slowly, looking in the windows, taking in every detail. Texas. This would have to be one of Barb's daughters. She had raised two daughters if he remembered correctly and they would both be adults by now. Barb had settled down in Texas. Oh he remembered that scandal. And Barb, his blood burned a little bit when he thought about her. He had been the spirit that watched over her from the moment she had been born here in this house. She had been the cutest and most precious thing he had ever seen or loved. He had been her childhood companion and her ghost playmate. He had watched out for her more than her or her parents had ever known. Emotion was bottling up inside him again, she had only ever hated him for it. Why hadn't she been able to understand him? Why hadn't she ever appreciated his presence in her life? Why had she rejected him so many times and so thoroughly?

He had tuned up her car when she was a teenager and of course she loved the way it drove, loved the power and the way it handled. He often rode with her to watch out for her. Sometimes he rode to high school with her in the morning and spent the day in town at the old fuel station and then he was waiting for her when she started up the car to drive home. All the pain seared inside his spirit when he remembered one particular morning when she had seen him in the passenger seat and pulled over to rebuke him. "Get out! Go home! Go home right now!"

She had yelled and pointed her finger like she was commanding an errant golden retriever. His ghost eyes had burned hot and dark and he had adjusted his felt cowboy hat leisurely before getting out with as much dignity as he could muster before she left him in the dust. That car really did move.

Or the time in third grade when the kids had been picking on her, saying terrible things about Ivory and Clyde. He had lost his temper and stood up for her. Had she ever thanked him for that? No. No one ever did. Everyone had over reacted. The kids, the teacher, Barb, her dad and especially her mom- all of them had blamed him for that unhappy day.

He realized with a pang that he still loved Barb. He would love that precious baby, that fierce little girl, that brazen woman he was so proud of for the rest of his haunted existence. Heck he had practically raised her. So there was no point staying mad at Barb. The night was progressing on as the ghost stewed and reminisced and circled the car and stared.

IV

Part Four

22

Good Night

The Heartless Ranch, Nebraska
   March of 2025

Emmy started watching a movie on her phone. She could never decide what movie to watch but 90's romantic comedies were usually a safe bet. She felt someone watching her. Willing herself to keep her eyes on her phone she coached herself internally, don't be paranoid, there is no one around. People go camping all the damn time, how is this any different?

She snuggled her face down into her bear. Something was watching her, probably an owl. Then she opened her eyes and stared out the dark view outside the passenger side window. The open space around her was lit by moonlight. Nothing to see, the wind continued to howl. She closed her eyes firmly and pressed her lips tightly together and clutched her fluffy pink bear in a death grip, feeling like a girl in a lifeboat out in the ocean in the eye of a hurricane. Doubling down her resolution, battered and tired she WOULD still be afloat in the morning.

Ashley hadn't gamed since before her last project. She kept making mistakes and her online gaming friends were starting to tease her. High in the Dallas nighttime skyline Ashley felt alone. Would Emmy be okay? She tried in vain to immerse herself in the game. Would her mom be okay? She eyed her phone, how long would it be before David texted her again. Before she really had to start packing? Ashley took off her headset and flopped face down on her bed.

Barb stayed at her gallery late that night, long after it had closed. She sat on the floor in an obscure corner, knees bent in front of her with surprising agility for her age, drinking a beer. She had left the main gallery lights off and only the accent lights illuminated the artwork and the spacious emptiness between the pieces. Her glasses were folded neatly on the marble floor beside her, she rubbed her face and the pain in her forehead. She sighed and it echoed around the modern space.

"Mom?"

She whispered.

"What do I do?"

Barb started to cry but stopped herself when she thought of all the eye makeup and liner, her false lashes. She sighed again instead. The immediate question at hand was her daughter and her daughter's safety. Barb considered the stacks of bracelets on her wrists and admitted to herself, Emmy would be fine. After all, she had survived.

Barb outlined the design on a particularly distinctive bracelet with the forefinger of the other hand. This piece had been made specifically for her and her situation by a tribal shaman when she toured Africa. She couldn't even remember what tribe, region or year, all her life experiences had been put in a blender recently. Nothing mattered now except her daughters. Still she had survived for years and years, Emmy would survive for a few days. Maybe she would even come home.

The questions she was grappling with now were the ones that were difficult to put into words, ones that she had repressed for decades. Why me, just didn't cover it. Why her parents-why what? Why were they who they were? Why did they do the things they did? She had been down all these thought trails too many times to count and that wasn't the real question that she wanted to ask. Barb pressed her forehead and again and willed her brain to stop churning. Tilting her head back against the wall she closed her eyes and slowly whispered aloud.

"I miss you two."

Then her cell phone jangled in her handbag and she cussed and spilled her beer. Ashley was calling. How late was it? She answered quickly while trying to remember if she had seen paper towels behind the front desk.

"Hey sweetie, you are lucky I didn't pee my pants."

23

Good Morning

The Heartless Ranch, Nebraska
  March of 2025

When the sun rose the light beams fell on Emmy in her little Malibu. And on Ashley, still collapsed face first on top of her white duvet. And technically on Barb, though due to the black out shades she slept on.

Emmy was so stiff when she stepped out of her car that she nearly fell down. The wind had finally stopped. She had such a headache. She sneezed, might be pollen allergies. She stopped to stretch and inhale deeply for a while, the air was so noticeably clean here. This all felt so new, nothing from last night could have been real. Emmy was starting to think about coffee and breakfast and all the exciting things she was looking forward to. This could be her home, her very own home. She owned this house. No one could sell it or make her leave. She looked at the structure approvingly, it had so much potential. Then she saw a cat, a kitten.

There was a kitten playing near the front step, she watched for a while. He was an all white kitten with two black front paws. Almost like he had stepped into black paint in a deep tray. She had never seen a kitten with markings like that. His all white face made him look like such a character. He seemed friendly but he was slow to let her pet him. Eventually Emmy picked him up.

"Well, hello."

She felt the purring through her fingers.

"Meow."

He must be a stray, she wished she had something to feed him.

The sun was getting warmer. Emmy started to rub her eyes then realized, no tears. No tears yesterday or last night, even though it was difficult. She smiled to herself. A plan was starting to formulate. Mr. Hammond had said the water was on and the plumbing in the house should be good to go, so Emmy eased into the house almost on tiptoe and used the bathroom. She was trying to look at everything and trying not to look at anything all at the same time. She felt like a National Geographic explorer or an anthropologist having been dropped into a foreign environment and time. Everything here potentially meant something to her, to her family's past and to her future. Last night when she had seen the blanket lying on the armchair it had freaked her out and she didn't want to encounter a similar scenario and have the same reaction again. So, she needed breakfast and she wanted to see the nearest town and know what was available to her.

Bumping back down the narrow lane from her house and back

to the highway Emmy felt a swell of pride, her house. This was going to be a good day. She wished the radio in her car worked, she felt like finding the local radio station and singing along. Then she thought of her mom, the radio didn't work because the radio stopped working in every single car her mom rode in. Emmy paused mentally to wonder when her mom ever would have ridden with her. Still no text messages or voicemails from her mom, that was something to be grateful for- but was her mom not speaking to her? How long would that last? Should she call her? Let her know that she was doing okay? No, Ashley would tell her. This was going to be such a good day, she needed music. Emmy looked at the broken radio again. Oh well, that was what her phone was for.

24

This Is Dismal

Dismal, Nebraska
  March of 2025

Thirty minutes later she saw the most extraordinary hand painted billboard in a little field of tall grass.

"This Is Dismal."

She saw broncs and floral flourishes and vintage lettering and soft color palettes and scenes of yuccas and clouds and grazing cattle and horses. What a piece of artwork.

The highway eased her around a bend and right into the center of the cowboy town of Dismal. The spring air was exhilarating so she rolled down her car windows a little and drove around slowly.

There was a little grocery store with a big sign advertising a coffee shop, they must be very proud of their coffee shop. She couldn't wait to be their customer but she wanted to know what all was in this town first. She could make plans over breakfast if she knew what her options were, so she drove up and down each and every street.

There was a gas station with four old fashioned pumps, two of which were still in use. The ruins of an old school gas station garage sat next to a newer, practical little stucco building. Sun light was draping through the ruined roof of the old structure and out the squares where panes of glass had been. The pillars and overhang were still in place, it was sad and phenomenal all at the same time. Emmy didn't stop to take a picture.

There was a little bitty bank and a teeny tiny post office. The courthouse and high school and elementary school were marked with their patriotic flags. A church and the cemetery looked out over the flat and the grass covered hills towering in the distance with a couple dozen houses nearby.

At the livestock feed store grain elevators towered into the sky and trucks were loading and unloading, corn dust rising high into the air. A vet clinic with pickups and trailers in the parking lot. This was clearly an agricultural hub. This was cowboy country. No, this was a cow town.

There was a bar with a large gravel parking lot on the outskirts of one side of town and a run down motel, with broken neon of a bronc rider under a moon and an assortment of flowerpots in the playful shapes of animals set out expectantly in the spring light, and across the highway a towering wooden grandstand in front of a rodeo arena.

Going back the other way on what must have been main street

but was now a paved highway she saw lots of boarded up buildings that she had missed the first time around. She eyed the trim work and the architectural styles, money had been spent here, a long time ago. This was a place full of a proud history. On the other edge of town she found a self proclaimed butcher block and a very brand new looking dollar store. That dollar store would be useful, this place was going to have everything she would need.

Emmy was surprised to see two chiropractor offices and one massage sign. These people must take their alternative medicine seriously. One chiropractor was in a new building on main street, near the bank and the post office. Emmy was surprised to see that the official looking sign offered energy healing. The massage sign had been in front of a house on a residential street. The third chiropractic sign had been in front of an old trailer house on the edge of town. She had even seen a nursery with greenhouses and a large spray painted sign that read "Rock Shop" in front of the roughest man made structure Emmy had ever seen. Underneath the large sign was a small sign that read "The Crystal Cowgirl" and Emmy grinned, she might really fit in around here. She could even start sketching up some landscape and garden plans today.

Emmy also noted a forlorn cafe with a big closed sign taped in the window. That left the grocery store coffee shop as the place to eat.

Still, this town had a lot more going on than the dozens of skeletal deserted dots on the map she had driven through to get here. This place was humming with business. She saw pickups with dogs on the back and pickups pulling trailers, she could see the horses' ears peeking out the top, and men in cowboy hats. She even saw men and women wearing chaps. She noticed a lot of people staring at her and she decided to smile and wave as calmly and positively as she could. Then she realized she must look like a wreck and checked her eye makeup in the rear view mirror, not as bad as it could have been. Oh, the front seat and the back of her car were still stuffed to overflowing with all her worldly possessions, so it was obvious to these people that she was moving. They probably thought she was lost.

25

The Dismal Grocery

Dismal, Nebraska
  March of 2025

When Emmy pulled open the door of the grocery store with the coffee shop sign a wonderful new world washed over her. The smell of freshly ground coffee beans, the sound of high heeled cowboy boots and spurs as someone strode over the polished cement floor, a baby cooing and women laughing. Emmy stopped, these were open, loud and unrestrained laughs. She had never thought about it before but so many women laughed with insecurity and restraint. Maybe she was really going to fit in here.

This place was clean. It was an open one room building, from the front door she could see everyone in the store. She could still smell hints of new construction, but it was the opposite of fancy. The floors were cement and the metal racks of groceries were sparsely stocked and widely spaced. Standard grocery store coolers and a row of basic home use freezers lined the back three walls. There were lots of windows that reached to the ceiling and the sun was pleasant in here, like a solarium, and three ceiling fans beat out a slow persistent rhythm. Large potted plants flourished throughout, maybe that was what made it feel like a greenhouse, and there were patio tables and chairs grouped in one corner.

At the front counter Emmy appreciated the hours of chalk board artistry that had gone into the enormous coffee shop type menu on the wall behind the counter. How tired she was started to show as she strained to read and decipher, lots of words but really basic options seemed to be the name of the game. Her eyes fell down from the sign to the woman in front of her and Emmy's eyes accidentally locked into hers. God she must look a terrible mess, the woman just stared and stared.

"What can I get for you honey?"

"Ummmm, that blended ice one please, caramel, large, do you have an extra large? With three shots of espresso please. Actually four."

The coffee shop woman in boots looked like she wanted to say something but got busy with the coffee instead. Emmy watched, rooted to the spot, this place felt so warm and safe. Coffee shop woman stopped the blender.

"Four shots, huh? Are you looking to fly without wings?"

Then she laughed at her own joke and fired up the blender again. Emmy couldn't help but join in with a laugh. If only this woman knew. Soon she was back, that looked like heaven in a tall clear plastic cup she was holding, individually wrapped straw in the other hand.

"That'll be $5.80, do you need anything else today?"

Something clicked in Emmy's mind. This place smelled like Lysol concentrate disinfectant, the same cleaner her mom had used growing up and still did to this day. That was where the nostalgia was coming from. Oh and she also needed cat food.

"Um, do you have any Lysol cleaner?"

The woman looked puzzled for a moment, but not over the inventory of cleaning products, she was a stocky woman with a well lined face, pretty earrings and large calloused hands.

"I'm sure we do, right this way."

They strode to the back corner of the store and the grocery store woman handed her the familiar dark bottle.

"I use this stuff here in the store, personal favorite, it's the only known disinfectant to kill tuberculosis."

She paused.

"Not that we need that, but I think it will solve about any dirt problem in existence." She laughed out loud again. Emmy smiled.

"Well I'm going to need it, I am going to start cleaning out my grandpa's house today."

The noise level in the store dropped perceptively. Emmy looked around her compulsively without turning her head. Then looked back at her new grocery store friend who was leaning forward to stare at her and speak thoughtfully.

"I feel like I should know you."

Her new friend broke the silence that had set in across the store.

"Who was your grandpa sweetie?"

"Um, Clyde Donahue-"

Emmy stammered.

"Ah! I knew it! I knew it. You look just like your mom. Just like her! I went to school with her! You probably don't know who I am, I'm Kathy White."

Emmy found herself shaking Kathy's man hand vigorously.

"Oh, I just can't get over it, you look just like she did at your age. How is your mom?"

"Um she's good–"

Emmy started walking toward the cash register with her Lysol in hand. Inner turmoil was mounting, she had never imagined that local people would know her mom, or her. How could she have been so stupid? Of course everyone here would know her grandpa and her mom. They would probably know them better than she did. Actually they would absolutely know her grandpa better than she did. In some ways every local person would know more about her own story than she did. Maybe her mom had been right.

Emmy wanted to bolt outside and drive back to Dallas, possibly throwing up a couple times on the gravel outside en route. She settled for putting one hand on her tummy. They were back at the front cash register, Emmy realized she hadn't been listening to Kathy's last few questions and Kathy was looking at her again.

"Sweetie, you look like you need to eat something. If you wait a little bit the noon meal today is beef and noodles, that might do you about as much good as anything. Oh and if you drink all that espresso on an empty stomach. Don't do that to yourself. Here let me get you some water and a snack and we'll sit down for a while. Jodi has the food all ready to go, she won't mind and in about a half an hour we will serve it up."

Kathy had been right about the food. Emmy had never tasted anything so good in her life. She felt so much better after eating. But she still couldn't wait to get away from Kathy and all her questions. She could tell her new friend was a genuinely very nice and good person- but snoopy. Realizing that everyone she met here would know more about her than she did had rattled her confidence at first but as she started up her little car to head home she was feeling good about it all again. She had bought some groceries and some Lysol and some cat food and somehow she felt ready for anything.

The drive home was blissful, she was starting to notice more of the details around her. She drove by gentle herds of cows and calves grazing peacefully in the breeze. She laughed aloud at how cute the calves were. The watercolor clouds in all their majesty felt reassuring above her. The highway stretched out in front her car- scenic and gorgeous and empty with plenty of space for all of her and her emotions. There would never be a need to make herself small in this place, on any level.

26

Someone Is Watching Me

The Heartless Ranch, Nebraska
   March of 2025

When she put her car in park and took the keys out of the ignition it was go time. She had a solid afternoon to make this place her home before the sun set. With her phone blasting her "Emmy Needs To Get Shit Done" playlist she bounded up the steps and pried open the door.

Half an hour later she was stalled out in the living room. The kitchen was fine for tonight. The bathroom was functional, she really needed to thank Mr. Hammond for turning the water on before she got here. She was going to leave the bedrooms alone for the time being, so that just left the living room as a place to sleep. There was a two cushion love seat from the 90's that used to be tan or beige and was swayed in the middle. Mounds of horrible and dirty decorative pillows covered it, everything was so dusty. The windows were long and narrow and had blinds, lace curtains, solid curtains and more lace curtains all done in layers and every layer was drawn to keep the sun out. She had started to disturb all those layers and let the sun shine in but when the sneezing and coughing started she quit. Taking down all the window treatments would be it's own deal.

The room was lit by an overhead light fixture, one of the bulbs was out and the fixture was filled with dead bugs. There were two lamps, one by each recliner. And that was where she got hung up, clearly her grandfather had been sleeping in this recliner and here his blanket lay where he had tossed it down. Had he known he would never come home again? Had he known that would be the last time he would sleep or nap in his own home? Who had helped him get settled in at the nursing home? Had anyone been there to hold his hand when he died? She perched on the arm of the sofa and stared and stared at Clyde's recliner.

Across the small room the ghost sat in the other recliner and stared at her staring. He had one cowboy boot resting on the opposite knee and his hat tilted back as he rested his head against the back of the old chair. He didn't have any cigarettes right now. Was this girl seriously thinking of living here? Would she move things around? Would she get rid of this chair?

As if in answer to his question Emmy grabbed four of the most offensive lace and embroidery pillows and tossed them down on the horrible brown carpet. He started to cough from shock. How could she do that? Waves of pain shot through his limbs and he started to panic. Evidently changes in his physical environment would be physically painful to him.

Emmy grabbed and grabbed again and he started to cough violently and she stopped and looked right at him, her eyebrows furrowed down over her eyes. She really did mean business. Next she went to her car and brought in a giant pink bag from which she extracted a sheet and a couple blankets. Then she proceeded to make the poor old love seat up for herself as if she owned the place. While she was gone for another load from her car the ghost sat gingerly on her sheets and touched them carefully one hand on either side of him, trying to acclimate and take it in. He had not expected to be this sensitive. He usually slept on the love seat. He scampered when Emmy reappeared suddenly and set out her bed pillows and her pink bear and a pair of sweatpants and scuff house slippers.

He cowered behind Ivory's old recliner while she found a suitable outlet and plugged in her phone charger. Next she cleared a space on the small table next to Clyde's recliner by unceremoniously setting piles of things on the floor next to it. Newspapers, scraps of paper, antacid bottles, coffee cups, the remote, band-aid wrappers, empty prescription bottles, Vix, dirty handkerchiefs, a broken pocket knife, paper clips, spare change, dead bugs, ancient cough drops, none of it gave her pause as she deposited it all on the floor. The ghost was pressed against the wall for support, trying to take one moment at a time. He was rapidly realizing how difficult all of this change was going to be for him. He retreated outside into the cool evening air while Emmy set out two water bottles, a tiny battery-powered humidifier, her essential oils, a few small stones and crystals, some magazines, and a stash of granola bars. He wished he could see through the windows better. What was she doing now? Surely she wouldn't bother his chair?

Finally Emmy set a tiny little footstool in front of the love seat, changed into her sweatpants and slippers, put the hood up on her hoodie and sat down carefully. Then she shrugged to herself. Whatever, it would work for tonight. She would probably survive a few days of camping like conditions. Still no tears, still on the right track. Then she called Phoebe.

Phoebe picked up part way through the first ring, she was a ride or die type of friend.

"So how is it? How's the ranch? I missed you today."

"Um, it's good. Different than I expected. Um. Say, Phoebe, do you want to come stay with me?"

Phoebe was lying on her futon nestled in huge piles of dirty and clean laundry, reading a book and trying not to think about the art collection or Barb or the future of her career or her finances.

"Do you think you could come stay for a little while, just until I get settled in?"

Phoebe had rolled over onto her stomach. Here she was, trying not to think about Barb. Should she go see Barb's childhood home for herself? Phoebe rolled off the couch onto the floor. Absolutely. Maybe she could even do the artwork collection there.

"What do you mean- I can't live with you forever?"

Emmy started to laugh.

"Okay, fine. You can come live here forever."

"No, seriously. What's it like?"

Phoebe was mentally extracting her suitcase from the bottom of the closet.

"Well, I'm happy. I haven't cried at all. I think this is the right thing for me. But I'm pretty sure it is haunted. My mom was right about that."

Emmy's eyes slid around the room, saying it out loud had made her feel nervous.

"What makes you say so? Have you seen anything?"

Phoebe was now physically extracting her suitcase from the bottom of her closet.

"No. Nothing to worry about. It just feels like somebody is watching me."

"Gotcha. Well they probably are. Have you met any local people?"

Phoebe was wondering how many sketchpads she needed to bring.

Emmy launched into a long diatribe about Kathy and not realizing that everyone here would know her mom and granddad.

Before Emmy was done describing it all Phoebe was loading three wheeled suitcases into her Mustang.

27

Nora Is Wrong

Nora fixed Zoe a roast beef sandwich and chips for supper. Zoe was seated at the island scrolling on her phone. She asked her mom without looking up.

"Did you hear anything about Ms. Donahue today? Her name is Emmy, right?"

Nora looked up from the cutting board because she had.

"Well, I stopped into the store to get eggs and Kathy told me that she had just had lunch with our young land lady."

"What's she like?"

"Well Kathy said she looks just like her mom and that she's really tired. And kind of private. Imagine that."

Nora laughed. She had known Clyde to be a very private individual but one of the truest friends to their family that she had ever known.

Zoe had more questions.

"How did it go last night?"

147

"That's all I know. But she must have gotten through the first night okay."

"Are you going to call her? Shouldn't we check on her?"

Zoe asked questions around bites of sandwich.

"I think I will give it a few days. I thought about it a little more and I think your Dad is right, she probably knows her business."

28

Don Goes For A Drive

The Heartless Ranch, Nebraska
  March of 2025

Emmy was starting to drift off to sleep. Don leaned against the cased opening between the living room and the kitchen, peering around the corner at her with his hat pulled down over his eyes. She had left all the lights on and her phone lay charging on the carpet. She had tossed and turned and stared at the ceiling and talked on the phone with Ashley for hours. The ghost thought she might stay up all night. But she had had a very long day and around one her eyelids dropped shut. Don crept across the living room to spend the night in his favorite green recliner. It's days might be numbered.

That afternoon while she had been gone he had located Clyde's old favorite flashlight and put new batteries in it for her. He was a little amazed that he had been able to do it. Being able to do things was such a thrill. As he passed by the love seat he set the flashlight on the foot stool but it rolled and fell to the dusty carpet. Emmy stirred but did not wake up.

Around 2 AM the ghost remembered Emmy's car and sat up with a start. He had been in suspense waiting to get a better look at it. He was so excited that he disappeared out of the recliner and reappeared by the driver's side door. A 2001 Chevy Malibu, a sad little four door car with chipped silver paint, it had been used hard and the ghost guessed that Emmy had not given very much for it. She would be thrilled when he was done. He popped the hood and was able to grip everything he wanted to. He laughed with glee as he checked the oil. Then he started to run his spirit eyes over every component, running his fingertips here and there and changing into pure spirit form to go inside first the engine and then the transmission and then the radiator and the fuel tank. Emmy snorted in her sleep inside the house on her love seat and rolled over pulling her blanket higher over her shoulders.

Don the ghost reappeared in front of the car and slammed the hood. He was pleased with his night's work. He opened the driver's side door to look at the gauges and gripped the steering wheel in one hand. A sudden rush of longing overtook him as he felt the firm grip and the tangible physical existence of the steering wheel. He was feeling so much stronger than normal, closer to having a physical form. He laughed robustly and slid into the driver's seat. Then staring at the gauges the realization hit him: this car had gas in the tank.

Don pulled his hat down over his eyes, grinning broadly as the little silver car rumbled over the auto gate and down the driveway toward the highway just before the darkness started to slowly ease into the first glimmers of sunrise. Emmy was getting into a good snoring rhythm and slept on completely unaware that her little car had been stolen.

29

How Was Your Night

The Heartless Ranch, Nebraska
March of 2025

The sun was up when a different car parked in front of the leaning picket fence. Emmy's eyes popped open, it was morning, someone was here. Oh wow my back hurts. She hurried to stand up and kicked the flashlight on the floor with her toe. Where had that come from? She wondered about it as she stumbled toward the kitchen and to the front door. She had bad breathe, wow she needed to go to the bathroom. Who was here? She had not seen a flashlight like that anywhere. Emmy stood agape inside the kitchen looking through the glass and the shredded screen door. Her car was gone. And her beautiful friend Phoebe was pulling a heavy suitcase out of the trunk of her white Mustang. How had she gotten here so fast? She threw open the doors and stumbled out onto the step.

"Phoebe! Phoebe, how did you get here?"

Phoebe spread her arms wide as if to embrace the sky and her friend and this entire place. "I drove!"

"You drove. Like all night?"

"Yep."

Phoebe was taking it all in. This was Barb's childhood home, the subject of her dreams and her soon-to-be artwork collection.

"It took me days to get here! How fast did you drive?"

Phoebe walked stiffly up the front walk and put her arm around Emmy shoulder.

"Your top speed is 55 miles per hour and you stop to take pictures of birds and bugs and clouds and random people in posed arrangements against their will. I love you but yes, I drove all night and I'm here!"

Phoebe pivoted to take it all in.

"Didn't you drive here? Where's your car?"

Emmy felt a little sad inside.

"Well, it was there. I parked it right there last night."

Phoebe narrowed her eyes.

"Your car has been stolen? Did you lock it?"

"Um, yeah I think so. I usually do. The keys are in my bag. Let me go make sure."

Emmy returned with the keys in her hand. Phoebe was trying not to get distracted by all the things to look at in the kitchen. She could hear wind chimes.

"Well, other than that, how was your night? Do you still think this place is haunted?"

30

Mr. Hammond and Nora Drive Faster Than Normal

The Hammond Ranch, Nebraska
March of 2025

Nora answered the house phone in the kitchen on the second ring.

"Hello?"

"Hi, this is Emmy Donahue, I'm calling for James."

"Hi! This is Nora, his wife. How are you getting along over there?"

"Well– um pretty good. Except um, well my friend showed up here this morning and we are out here in the yard and– my car is missing."

Emmy sounded perfectly apologetic. Nora's ghost radar shot up so fast she almost hurt herself. Where was James? She looked about the kitchen even though she knew he had left in his feeding pickup.

"I think it might have been stolen. But that just seems so weird.

What do you think?"

Emmy was a total sweetheart, Nora could tell. Where was her husband?

"I just don't know, let me send James over there. He'll help you figure out what to do."

Nora didn't even say goodbye as she hung up the receiver and hurried to pull on her boots by the door. She hustled out across the yard and fired up her four wheeler and raced in pursuit of James in his feeding pickup trailing out into the dewy morning with a hot cup of coffee in hand. He didn't see her at first but then pulled to a stop immediately, had something happened to one of the kids? A few moments later James and Nora Hammond were headed over to the old Heart Seven south place, which they had leased for many years first from Clyde and then from his granddaughter. A place where they never kept vehicles or tractors.

James' cell phone rang as he pushed the loaded feeding wagon to a precarious forty miles an hour and the weight started to sway from side to side.

"It's Brian."

He handed the phone to Nora.

"Brian, it's mom, what's up?"

"There's a car over here behind the barn, it has Texas license plates. A little silver four door thing."

Brian paused. Nora could hear the tractor roaring away behind him.

"August told me the young Ms. Donahue is staying over on the south place. Is this her car?"

Brian sounded irritable.

He always sounded that way. He was an ambitious cattleman

in his prime with small children and not enough hours in the day.

Nora covered the cell phone receiver and leaned toward her husband beside her in the pickup.

"Brian found it. It's out back of the barn over there."

James nodded and turned the top heavy pickup around in a tight circle to go back the other way, toward the old Heart Seven headquarters where Brian lived.

Nora got back on the phone.

"Brian, would you go look in it and see if the keys are there?"

They weren't. James turned the pickup around again and headed back south to Clyde's old place.

Emmy and Phoebe were sitting on the cement step eating the donuts Emmy had brought home from the grocery store yesterday when a beat up pickup truck came up the drive a little too fast and a dignified older couple got out. Mr. Hammond was wearing modern sunglasses and a big tan overcoat. Nora had short chic hair and was struggling for composure. She seemed like the kind of woman who was normally very composed.

"We found it. It's over at our other place, behind the barn. It wasn't stolen. Do you have the keys? We can just drive it home."

Phoebe was also normally a very composed woman but she had been up all night.

"What do you mean? How did it get over there?"

Phoebe stood up.

"This doesn't seem right to me."

She stepped a little in front of Emmy defensively.

"What's going on?"

"Sorry, hi, I'm Nora Hammond."

She held out her hand but Phoebe didn't take it. Nora barreled on without hesitating.

"We lease the place from Emmy. Hi Emmy, nice to meet you." Emmy shook her hand politely.

"And um, I'm sure you've heard that this place is haunted. Probably your mom told you? And sometimes vehicles, you know, go missing, get driven away. It's something we've had a lot of over the years. James tells me that the ghost, um was a mechanic, loved cars."

Nora explained all of this the way a parent explains to a mortified Sunday school class why their child just threw up.

Phoebe and Emmy stared at her openly.

V

Part Five

31

Barb's Secret

Dismal, Nebraska
  March of 2025

The noon meal at the grocery store that day was sloppy joes with beans and potato chips. Phoebe and Emmy were seated cozily in the corner with all the plants and the patio tables and chairs. After going to retrieve Emmy's car from behind a barn the morning stretched on and the donuts started to feel like ages ago. Emmy could tell Phoebe liked this place too. She was perched happily on one of her special purple sitting cushions, on top of the patio chair's normal cushion. Phoebe was a very cool woman but she absolutely refused to tolerate tailbone pain or uncomfortable sitting.

"Life is too short."

She would exclaim bluntly to anyone that questioned her about this eccentricity.

"So, your mom's old house is haunted by a ghost that steals cars?"

Phoebe asked this around a mouthful of hot sandwich.

"This food is really good."

"I know-"

Emmy agreed with her wholeheartedly.

"Phoebe I'm worried about your Mustang."

That problem was not lost unto Phoebe but she smiled smugly, she had seen a thing or three in her cross continental lifetime.

"I was too. But I think we are going to be okay."

Phoebe continued teasingly.

"Maybe the ghost will stay just as in love with your Malibu as you are."

Kathy and Jodi had paused as they washed the lunch dishes, hoping to hear more clearly. A cheerful bell chimed as someone in cowboy boots came in the front door.

When Brian Hammond introduced himself to Emmy and to Phoebe with a brusque handshake he clearly had business on his mind.

"I'm Brian Hammond, I live over on the old Heart Seven main place. And I'm very sorry about your car."

Emmy leaned over to check on it through the big windows in the front of the grocery store, it was still parked right out front.

"Oh I think we are good, but thank you."

"I'm not sure if my parents really explained the situation to you as well as they maybe should have. You need to know that your house there is known to be haunted. My dad thinks that you will be fine, safe. But I think you should know in full disclosure that we take it seriously enough that we don't leave any kind of vehicle or tractor over there, they get- relocated."

Brian looked to Phoebe to make sure Emmy was listening to

him but Phoebe had a question.

"Why did Emmy's car end up over at your place? I mean if this sort of thing has happened before, are there certain places the cars usually end up?"

Brian Hammond cast a glance out the big front windows, he had left his pickup running with two small children in it and three dogs on the back. He needed to remember to get a package of donut holes before he headed back out.

"I think, the spirit, goes to my place because they used to be two places on the same ranch. You know, your house there was the south place and where I live was the main place. Before Barb sold the main place to my dad. So it makes sense to me that he would be going there."

He lowered his voice a little more.

"We have also found vehicles here in town at the old filling station. And at the cemetery."

Brian Hammond straightened back up, duty to communicate fulfilled his mind was back on donuts and yearling steers in the pens.

"I'm sure my dad is right and you will be fine, but Laura and I wanted to make sure you knew everything. You can call me anytime."

He returned from the counter shortly with a scrap of paper.

"This is my cell phone number. And this is my wife Laura's cell phone number, I think she'd like to meet you two. And this is our house phone number. If anything, comes up."

With that he shook both their hands again and left Emmy and Phoebe over their lunch.

"Your mom sold a ranch to Mr. Hammond? Did you know that?"

Phoebe asked Emmy as they sat there, food forgotten.

"No- I didn't. I guess that's why my grandpa was so sure she would sell the rest of it. That makes sense."

"Why would she do that?"

Phoebe's voice trailed off as she asked the question. She suddenly understood how Barb had been able to launch her first gallery. Emmy was remembering her childhood along the Dallas skyline. Imagining a much younger version of her mom, raising two daughters alone in one of the nicest apartment buildings in the city. It all made sense. Her mom was always so grateful, had always been so grateful. Every time she touched a doorknob or a counter top that touch was silently imbued with gratitude. Her mom had sold the historic family property and bought a new life for herself. And her daughters.

Emmy looked at Phoebe.

"Do you think that's why she never spoke to her parents again? That would have to be the riff."

"Or maybe they never spoke to her again."

Emmy and Phoebe both felt suddenly, very sad. Phoebe's mind was working much faster than Emmy's though.

"But why did she own it in the first place? I mean how did she come to have it to sell? Evidently her parents still had some of it- and that's what they left to you."

Emmy wasn't really listening. In her mind's eye she saw the crocheted blanket tossed down on the recliner arm, as if their owner was coming back later. Her granddad had been living alone. He had been taken to the nursing home, had he been alone? His daughter never said goodbye to him before he died, had anyone been there to hold his hand? The pain of it all

164

welled up inside Emmy's chest. Surely she would have been by her mom's side? They hadn't spoken for a couple of days and her mom didn't want her to be here. Maybe the pattern was repeating itself. The pressure of it all was hurting her heart. And although Emmy didn't notice, there were still no tears.

When they got back to the ranch that afternoon Phoebe was starting to get very tired. Emmy put the Malibu in park and took the keys out of the ignition. Would her car be stolen again tonight? Maybe this was all a bad idea. The wind was picking up, the girls didn't know it but the barometric pressure was dropping and there would be rain that night. They did hear the crow, this was crow weather in Dismal.

"Ha! Cah... C...a-"

While Emmy carried the rest of Phoebe's things in Phoebe put a parking boot on her driver's side front tire. She had produced the thing proudly from a sports bag in the trunk of the car.

"I wish I had one for your car though."

She really was getting tired, she sounded wistful.

"I guess if it works I will get another one."

That night the two friends curled up together on the love seat in the living room in sweatpants and sweaters with hoods up. Rain pattered on the windows in the dark. They started a movie together on Emmy's phone but Phoebe fell asleep within minutes. Emmy was trying not to look at her granddad's old recliner, she had folded the blanket and placed it respectfully over the sagging arm of the chair.

She sent a text before she went to sleep.

"How are you doing mom? I miss you and I love you."

Emmy didn't know if that would make it worse or better but she felt better for having sent it and went to sleep.

In the green recliner across the narrow room from the love seat Don yawned and stretched. When Phoebe woke briefly in the night she thought she smelled cigarette smoke.

32

Crow Weather In Dismal

The Heartless Ranch, Nebraska
  March of 2025

This was crow weather in Clara County. The sun rose on a wet morning thick with fog and ethereal mist. Everyone wanted to sleep in but their dreams were filled with regrets and doubts so they got up and made coffee. Time moved more slowly today. The horses on the hills and in the meadows grazed slowly, each one an island in the clouds setting on the land. The forecast was calling for rain all day and storms in the evening.

Calving was in full swing at the Hammond ranch home place and at Brian's place. This had been a good calving year with stable weather so far. The air felt thick with a feeling of hard earned arrival- and allergies. Calves raced around playfully with their buddies. In late March the air is full of birds in love and avian glee. All the people were busy feeding hay to their cattle, pairing out and checking their heavies. Even the dirt was exuberant with a microscopic vitality.

Still there was a feeling of uneasy anticipation underneath it all- there was still potential for spring temperature drops and blizzards.

Emmy walked around her new old house with a cup of coffee, taking in the rainy views from the different windows through the grime and the cobwebs. Everything smelled so, alive. She had been here for over a week now. Phoebe had made short work at the new dollar store in Dismal and set up a basic coffee pot and some Styrofoam cups in the living room.

Phoebe was still asleep on the love seat this morning, she had her grounding mat plugged into an outlet across the room and the cord strung across the decaying carpet. Emmy thought the smell of coffee brewing might wake her but it hadn't. Emmy stepped slowly and carefully around the house, taking it all in. She ate peanut butter out of the jar for breakfast. That used to make Matt so crazy that she had stopped doing it when she was living with him. He would say she needed to take more time for food planning. Emmy stared in silence at the kitchen layout in front of her, the way the rainy light from the windows played across the surfaces. Everything smelled damp and musty, the coffee was a welcome counterpoint, underneath that Emmy thought she smelled cigarette smoke.

Phoebe had helped her etch out the barest path of existence in the last week. And it had been a good week. After the initial scare with the car they hadn't seen any more ghost activity. The nights had been very scary but the two of them slept in a pile under the blankets together on the love seat, Phoebe with her head on the south end and Emmy with her head on the north, and the silliness of it all had helped. Phoebe had the covers pulled over her shoulders when she spoke.

"You do realize this place is haunted as hell."

"I know. I'm sorry."

"Oh don't be. You know it doesn't feel bad. I thought it would feel, like bad places do."

"I know! Like obviously none of this is good, but it feels right to me. Kind of like sinking into a hot bath. What is that supposed to mean?"

"I don't know- Emmy, I dreamed your mom's dreams and made artwork about them."

Emmy was quiet for a while and pulled the covers up tighter.

"That must have been a trip."

"Well honestly I think I'm still on it. They were all about this place."

When Emmy spoke it was full of kindness.

"Do you think we are doing the right thing?"

"I do. I'm with you, this feels right. You own a house. You might as well live here if you want to. Maybe the ghost will move over after a while. Who knows."

"Well I guess."

"Actually probably not- but here we are."

They laughed with impunity and the sound rang out through the dark across the valley. It was hard to be scared of anything when Phoebe Laurent was your friend.

The kitten had taken to Phoebe instantly. Emmy was thrilled when she found a vintage red wicker cat basket with a little red cushion at the end of the love seat in the living room. She had moved it out into the light from the window and Spot had taken to it instantly. That cat slept so hard. He was passed out on his back in the basket with his feet up in the air right now. She could just see the little white spot on the bottom of his black right paw. He still wouldn't eat any of the cat food she had bought for him. Phoebe rolled over sleepily on the love seat.

This felt like their beginning, a new story that belonged to Phoebe and Spot and herself. Emmy felt a surge of affection for them all. When she remembered her mom growing up here, right here and focused back in on all of her grandparent's possessions it felt a bit shocking. So many things to be addressed and resolved. Everything from their clothes to their false teeth to old appliances and photo albums and unopened mail. Emmy sipped her coffee, it would be difficult but she knew it was possible. This could be her home.

33

She Belongs Here

The Heartless Ranch, Nebraska
  March of 2025

Emmy sent a text to Ashley.

"Good morning, so rainy here."

She set down her coffee cup and took a picture out the front door and sent the picture too.

"The neighbors are coming over to help us clean today."

Emmy inserted a few emojis.

"I'm a little nervous."

Ashley was still sleeping and wouldn't get the texts until later.

Nora tapped on the front screen door and Emmy hurried to let her in.

Nora had started the morning by making homemade waffles and scrambled eggs for her family and serving coffee around the big dining room table with the lazy susan in the middle. It was all quite cozy in the rain and the fog. James had refused to comment on her plans for the day. Zoe had tried to stay home, pleading how tired she was and everything she needed to do and even invoking algebra homework. Nora was having none of it. In the end Zoe realized she wouldn't want to miss out on anything exciting that might happen with the ghost anyway. Beth was happy to be home and curious about the day ahead of them, the weather felt incredible to her. She wondered over her fifth cup of coffee if the bathroom worked over there or if she was going to spend the day running out into the rain. Nora was filling a second thermos full of coffee even as she wondered.

Nora, Beth and Zoe were soaked before they got inside the house but they didn't seem to mind. They looked around curiously, their wet shoes quickly turned the dirt and grime on the old linoleum into big slippery streaks. Each of the Hammond women was carrying a big laundry basket, luckily one of them included rolls of paper towels.

"Good morning Emmy, I hope you are ready to get after it. I hope we can get it all done today. Did you know where you wanted to start?"

Phoebe wandered in sleepily in her pajama bottoms, a sweat-shirt with a Korean character on the front and her house slippers with birds embroidered on them.

"Hi."

She waved sleepily.

Beth moved forward to shake her hand and soon the two of them were visiting in the living room over coffee.

"I don't know. Where do you think we should start?"

"Well kitchen and bathroom are always good but I don't know how we are supposed to clean with all this stuff in the way. Did you know what you wanted to do with any of it?"

Emmy was feeling more incompetent by the question. The truth was a bit counter-intuitive, she felt it would be wisest to move as little as possible.

"I hadn't really thought about it."

She replied, slightly apologetic.

Zoe watched the discourse the way one watches a tennis match.

Nora forged on, younger women were often clueless, she had two daughters to illustrate her point.

"Well I guess it depends on how you want to use the space. Are you planning on being here this winter? What room do you want for your bedroom? James tells me you work from home, had you thought about setting up a home office space? I don't know what you need."

Zoe was used to be the focus of her mom's strict ramrodding but she felt a little bad for Emmy. She could hear laughter in the living room and wondered what she was missing in there.

"I think, I need another cup of coffee. Let me ask Phoebe." Emmy pivoted politely out of the questions and moved to join Phoebe in the living room and invoke her opinion.

"Phoebe, have you thought about what bedroom you want?"

Phoebe could hear the broken wind chimes outside. She felt a thrill of recognition from her dreams. Who was the ghost that haunted this place? She could tell Beth was a natural teacher, she felt like she had known her forever already. Maybe she could answer some of their questions but she didn't know what questions to ask. The pace of the rain was picking up outside, a crow cawed violently just outside the living room window.

"I don't know, it's pretty creepy around here at night. Maybe we'll just stay in the living room for now."

Beth and Zoe looked at each other knowingly, they were both impressed and intimidated by these cosmopolitan women from Dallas. Imagine spending the night in this wreck of a haunted house. Emmy and Phoebe did not seem perturbed. Beth and Zoe looked at each other knowingly again, Emmy and Phoebe weren't western at all but they were clearly as bad and wild as the west itself.

Nora was starting to question the fate of humanity as she looked at the four of them. They weren't going to get a dang thing done today. Zoe could tell her mom was getting impatient. Beth wanted to plop down on the love seat, coffee cup in hand in the soft rainy light and have them tell her everything. Zoe knew it was up to her. So she spoke for the first time since they arrived.

"What if, we stacked all these things from these rooms into one of these bedrooms." Zoe gestured to the two doors behind her leading off the living room.

"And set up kind of a shared living area here in the living room."

Phoebe and Beth were nodding. Zoe continued in her shy teenage voice.

"We could box up everything from the kitchen and bathroom and store it and then we'd be able to clean."

Zoe looked to her mom for approval and found it. She felt very proud.

"Who's this?"

Beth was picking up a stretching Spot out of his cat basket.

"His name is Spot."

Emmy explained as she stood close by to pet the purring kitten in Beth's arms. Zoe and Nora stared at her. This was a very unusual looking, all white cat with two black- mittens. Phoebe snorted into her coffee.

"Well he's adorable."

Beth bopped his nose gently, irony lost unto her. Phoebe smiled in spite of herself, Beth and Emmy were going to get along really well. Then Nora was handing her an empty cardboard box.

Phoebe decided to pack things up from around the piano. This was the piano from her dreams and she was drawn to it. Pianos are orderly sorts of musical instruments. Black and white keys, no gray areas. Each note clearly designated and organized. She had never thought about it much until lately. Why was the piano in the dream? What did the dreams mean? Was the ghost trying to tell her something all those weeks ago? The hairs on her arms stood up as she wondered if she would hear the piano playing one evening. No, they had seen no more ghost activity and besides, this ghost was into cars. Phoebe shifted uneasily as she remembered the car without a driver. Phoebe could hear Emmy exclaiming to Beth in the kitchen over the wallpaper and welcomed the distraction.

The wallpaper had surprised Phoebe. In her dreams the daisies had been in a bouquet and then in a field. In reality they were a pattern on sun bleached peeling wallpaper splattered with grease and black with grime. Emmy was into it though, she had taken tons of pictures. She found the vintage-ness of the floral pattern energizing. Her enthusiasm really was contagious. Phoebe was packing stacks of magazines and newspapers into boxes. There was unfinished knitting and boxes of pills and doilies and figurines galore. Behind a decaying cardboard box full of sheet music and hymnals she found the radio. It was a basic weather emergency battery powered radio with an antenna and knobs on the front. Phoebe's heart felt heavy as she held the physical version of her vision in her hands. This wasn't all a movie or a story or a daydream, this was real. She nestled the radio carefully in the load and when another crow cawed she looked out the window, hoping to see it. It sounded so close by.

Zoe watched her discreetly from where she was packing up Clyde's recliner side table belongings. She remembered Clyde, she had been in elementary school at the time- but she remembered him. He had died of lung cancer. They had all been at this funeral. Her parents had known him very well. Zoe watched Phoebe put her long silky black hair up in a clip and thought she was an incredibly beautiful and sexy woman. She wondered what it was like to be totally grown up and on your own.

Emmy had moved into showing Beth all of her favorite discoveries around the house. Beth was all too happy to share in her journey of enthusiasm. Zoe listened as Emmy exclaimed over a green chair at the kitchen table. Evidently the shade was avocado green, from the 70's and the white floral pattern on it was dainty while surprisingly graceful for how energetic it was. Zoe leaned a little to see the chair through the cased opening with new eyes. Her sister Beth's rear end was in the way.

Zoe was rolling up the length of tubing from one of Clyde's oxygen tanks. Now she could hear Emmy verbally appreciating the telephone on the wall. Her voice rang with admiration.

"Seems so formal and significant, like making a phone call

has some weight to it."

Zoe pictured the black rotary phone with the long spiral cord hanging down the wall, it likely was pretty heavy.

"It probably still works."

Beth added helpfully. Then she added an after thought.

"Well I'm sure the phone line is disconnected, but the telephone itself probably still works."

"Did you see these phone numbers?"

Emmy had moved on.

There was a tattered piece of paper taped on the wall next to the phone. Perfectly ornate and tilting cursive had written telephone numbers in pencil, it seemed like an eerie link to another time and place. The person who wrote those phone numbers so painstakingly was long gone from this place but their handwriting left an undying presence, like they might be back at any moment.

"Oh look, this is my grandma. Doris Hammond."

Beth laughed before she continued.

"That's still our land line number, over at the house."

Zoe and Phoebe were listening carefully, each in their own little world. The rain poured on. Nora chimed in from where she was packing things in the bathroom.

"They were friends. Your grandma Doris Hammond and Gladys Donahue. Friends and neighbors."

Spot the cat chirped happily from his perch on top of the old green recliner. Phoebe patted his head playfully.

Beth and Phoebe had moved on to the decorative items hanging on the wall in the kitchen next to the phone.

"These things always look so creepy."

Beth was having a wonderful time.

Zoe and Phoebe gave up their efforts and went to go look. It was a ceramic plaque painted by a child, depicting the face of Jesus in prayer. Zoe had seen them before but Phoebe thought it was downright bizarre looking, the colors were garish. Nora had come to join them, loaded box on her hip.

"Oh everyone has those, back in the day all the kids painted them in Sunday school."

Emmy reached out to take it down and pack it away and found that it was glued to the wall. She couldn't budge it. With a pang Emmy remembered her mom, had her mom painted that plaque in Sunday school? She moved on to contemplate a beautiful poem below the strange ceramic plaque.

Footprints in the Sand
  One night a man had a dream.
  He dreamed he was walking along the
  beach with the Lord.
  Across the sky flashed scenes from his life.
  For each scene, he noticed two sets of
  footprints in the sand; one belonging to
  him, and the other to the Lord.
  When the last scene of his life flashed
  before him, he looked back at the
  footprints in the sand.
  He noticed that many times along the
  path of his life there was only one set
  of footprints.
  He also noticed that it happened at the
  very lowest and saddest times in his life.
  This really bothered him and he questioned
  the Lord about it.

"Lord, you said that once I decided to follow
you, you'd walk with me all the way.
But I have noticed that during the most
troublesome times in my life there is only
one set of footprints.
I don't understand why when I needed
you most you would leave me."
The Lord replied, "My precious, precious child,
I love you and I would never leave you.
During your times of trial and suffering, when
you see only one set of footprints in the sand
it was then that I carried you."
-Author Unknown

"Have you read this?"

Emmy asked Beth.

"Oh yeah, I think everyone's grandma had a copy of that.
Probably right next to these Sunday school plaques."

"What do you think it means?"

Emmy narrowed her eyes, reading it again.

Beth pondered, her first year at the university wasn't going
particularly well.

"I think everyone goes through some hell on earth, if you will.
No matter who you are. But some of us have more help than we
realize."

Nora was throwing open the kitchen cupboard doors.

"Do you want any of these dishes left out?"

In the end Emmy wanted all of them left out. Her grandmother
had been into color and pattern and animal motifs. Emmy had

never seen anything like it. Then she saw the recipe cards taped on the inside of the dirty white cupboard doors. They were weathered and stained and some were so faded the writing was barely legible. Most of them seemed to have something to do with gelatin.

"Jello must have really been a thing, huh?"

Nora was wiping Pyrex after Pyrex down with a damp rag. She at least wanted to get that top layer of caked on dirt off before Emmy tried to eat off them. She was using hot water and Lysol disinfectant in an old ice cream bucket, she had uncovered a lifetime supply of Lysol cleaner stashed under the kitchen sink and decided to go ahead and use it, in honor of old Clyde.

"Oh yes, layered Jello, Jello in a fancy dish, Jello molds, Jello with fruit or marshmallows, or both. There's just a lot you can do with it and it was very popular. I still make that kind of thing sometimes."

"Is it good?"

Emmy asked curiously. Phoebe was wondering the same thing.

"Oh it's very good. My kids liked it. Easy to make, cheap, kind of bright and refreshing- light."

"Probably kind of good for you too if it didn't have so much sugar in it, my dad would have lived off of Jello if he could have."

Nora added her reminiscence as an after thought. All this nostalgia was getting to her.

"We should make these recipes!"

Emmy looked so excited all four women were sure she meant right now.

"That sounds fun! Jello is really good."

Beth was totally onboard.

Orange Jello
   One box orange jello.
   2 cans mandarin oranges.
   Marshmallows.

Drain the juice from the mandarin oranges and set aside. Prepare Jello according to box, substitute juice for some of the water. Place mandarin oranges in the bottom of the dish, pour the liquid over the top of the fruit. Refrigerate. Add marshmallows to the top after the Jello has started to set up.

When the three Hammond women left that afternoon the house was still a wreck but it could now pass as a place where living people lived.

   "She's dingy. I give it three months."

Nora was still frustrated. Zoe was looking out the pickup window at the rain.

   "You're wrong Mom. She belongs here."

Beth was wondering if she would ever live somewhere cosmopolitan like Dallas.

Don watched them leave from under the eaves of the barn.

   "Mom! I see him! I think I saw him-"

Zoe had caught a glimpse of his hat and silhouette in the shadows through the rain. Nora stopped and they all stared for a while. But they didn't see anything.

About the Author

Bunny Hammond is a pen name for the This Is Dismal series. The author lives in Nebraska with her husband and children. She is very happy to have finished writing her first novel. Thank you for reading.

Please consider reviewing this novel. Reviews are very important in the book world and yours would make a difference.

If you would like to be notified when new novels in this series are released please sign up for the newsletter using the link below or by going to the Bunny Hammond website. Bunny dislikes email overload so she has no plans to spam you. Thank you.

You can see the colors and patterns of Dismal on the Bunny Hammond website, in social media and on Spoonflower.

You can connect with me on:

🌐 http://www.bunnyhammond.com

🅵 https://facebook.com/61571334758010

𝒆 https://www.pinterest.com/bunnyhammond

𝒆 https://www.instagram.com/bunnyhammond23

𝒆 https://www.spoonflower.com/profiles/bunnyhammond

𝒆   https://www.goodreads.com/book/show/220172466-the-heartless-ranch-is-haunted

Subscribe to my newsletter:

✉ https://www.bunnyhammond.com/newsletter

Also by Bunny Hammond

Coming Soon: The second novel in the This Is Dismal series, entitled This Is Dismal- Welcome Home.

This Is Dismal
Welcome Home.

www.ingramcontent.com/pod-product-compliance
Lightning Source LLC
Chambersburg PA
CBHW070514260626
47161CB00004B/1543